Free to Fall

THE FREEMAN BROTHERS

CHESAPEAKE HEIGHTS
BOOK ONE

LOUISE LENNOX

AFROCHANT

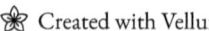 Created with Vellum

Blurb

She's his greatest temptation. He's her biggest risk. Together, they just might fall...

Jabari

Love? I don't do that anymore. I've had my fill of betrayal, of trusting the wrong people, of letting my guard down only to be burned. My life is about control now—running the Freeman family empire, upholding our legacy, and keeping my heart locked behind walls no one can break.

Then *she* shows up.

Sierra Watson is nothing like the women I've known—bold, beautiful, and completely unimpressed by me. She challenges me, meets my sharp edges with smooth confidence, and refuses to be anything less than herself. I should stay away. I *need* to stay away. But when she looks at me, I feel something shift, something crack open that I thought was long dead.

But love has cost me before, and I can't afford to lose again.

Sierra

I don't have time for love. Not when my family is depending on me. Not when my sister's reckless decisions have forced me into a second job I never wanted, working for the powerful Freeman family to clean up a mess I didn't make.

Then I meet *him.*

Jabari Freeman is infuriating—cold, controlled, and way too arrogant for his own good. He pushes, I push back. But the more I fight it, the harder it becomes to ignore the fire between us. And when that fire ignites, it's impossible to put out.

But love has never come without sacrifice for me. And just

when I think I might finally have something for myself, the life I've been trying to escape comes crashing back in.

Jabari has his own demons to fight, and I have mine. The question is... *are we strong enough to fight for each other?*

🔥 **Enemies-to-lovers tension** 🔥 **Irresistible chemistry** 🔥 **Steamy Small Town Romance** 🔥 **A love worth risking everything for**

Set against the lush backdrop of Southern Maryland's Chesapeake Heights, ***Free to Fall*** is a soulful story of resilience, redemption, *featuring the Freeman family. This is Book One: Jabari's Story.*

To K,
The man who made my small-town fantasies come true!

Rest in Heaven Nikki Giovanni

...I love you
        because you made me
            want to love you
        more than I love my privacy
            my freedom   my commitments
                and responsibilities
    I love you 'cause I changed my life
            to love you
        because you saw me one Friday
            afternoon and decided that I would
    love you
    I love you I love you I love you

-Excerpt from **Resignation** by Nikki Giovanni

ONE

Careless Whisper

JABARI

HOME IS WHERE THE HEART IS—OR SO THEY SAY.

But I left my heart here in Chesapeake Heights to wither and die ten years ago. Now, I'm back for my father's funeral, and as my sleek black F-150 glides silently down the crowded boardwalk of my coastal hometown—its electric motor as quiet as the ache in my chest—I can feel every set of eyes on me.

Chesapeake Heights doesn't forget, and neither do its people. My return is the kind of thing that makes curtains twitch, and whispers rise like the tide.

That's because here, I'm not just Jabari Freeman, Chesapeake Height's infamous prodigal son; I am a bad omen, quietly wrapped in dark metal, returning home from my exile to mark the end of an era.

My beloved father's death.

When I left a decade ago, I was not quiet. I was loud and

violent as I stumbled from the scene of my naked fiancée being fucked into our Alaskan King bed by my best friend. I'd just returned from my third and final tour in Afghanistan as a SEAL. I wanted to surprise her a week early, finally ready to live the life I was destined to lead. I had her dream wedding ceremony planned on the beach in Hawaii, and our families prepared to meet us there.

My life plan was simple: marry Vanessa "Vee" Taylor, my high school sweetheart, and prepare to become the oldest Freeman son and take over Chesapeake Heights Beach Resort.

Instead, I beat my former best friend Jason Carrington into a bloody pulp and high-tailed it out of town. I reenlisted, and I haven't been back here since that day. Like always, my father had my back and ensured no charges were pressed against me.

For a moment, I thought about returning home and seeing if I could understand why Vee did it. I know the back-to-back deployments were hard on her; maybe we could find a way back to each other if I forgave her.

But Vee married that prick Jason a week later, and I was done.

Love wasn't for me. Women should be pleasured and cherished but never trusted. When I need a woman, I have no problem coaxing one to my bed because I'm richer than Midas from smart investing over the years, and I have a body that proves I am still a SEAL.

I also know my way around a woman's body, so my reputation often precedes me. No woman leaves my bed without coming at least three times.

We both get what we need and move on because I don't do relationships.

As I pass former neighbors, whispers of suspicion and awe stir in the breeze and slip through my open windows. I roll my eyes, knowing that gossip is the lifeblood of a small town, and right now, my family and I are the main event. But once the sun hits the jet-black skin of my forearm, resting casually on the open windowsill, I tune it all out and realize that a part of me is glad to be home.

"Hey there, Jabari!" Mr. Harrington calls out to me from his usual boardwalk bench, his hand raised in a wave that holds more pity than welcome. I give him the obligatory nod—a brief chin tilt that serves as my universal reply to the townsfolk who think they know me because they've watched me grow up.

As I press the gas pedal and the truck glides forward, the smell of freshly cut grass hits me, blending with the sweet, rich scent of blooming magnolias in full bloom. Their blossoms line the driveway like a sweet-smelling welcome mat, leading me back to Baycrest—our family home.

The old mansion comes into view, towering over the other houses nearby like it knows it's the star of the show. It's not just a house; it's a piece of us—our history, our pride, and maybe a little bit of our baggage too.

Its brick walls are dove-white, with white pillars and a large, ornate gold and haint-blue front door. The color is a nod to my ancestors' Gullah roots. The large windows are adorned with natural wood shutters, and the manicured lawn is bordered by the elegant hedges that our longtime gardener, Hector, is currently pruning to perfection. I shake my head as I park in our circular driveway; he's seventy-six years old and won't retire.

Arriving at Baycrest feels like stepping into another world— a blessing I can't entirely accept. This house, this grand estate, is the very heartbeat of Chesapeake Heights, the pulse that keeps the town alive. But with it comes a weight of regret; it presses down on me with a force I've never entirely been able to escape.

Chesapeake Heights is a coastal paradise where the waves whisper secrets to those who listen. And my family—my legacy —dominates nearly all of it. For over a century, we have owned

95 percent of the land, the cottages, and the very essence of this place. My father, his father, and his grandfather wore this crown with pride, each a guardian of our family's heritage.

But when it came time for me to take my place, to step into the role I was born for—I ran. I turned away from everything, from the expectations, from the legacy... all because of a betrayal that still stings, its scars deep and raw, refusing to fade with time. I always planned to return, but as the years passed, I couldn't face my family for being a coward or the broken heart I left here.

But I'm here now.

I cut the engine and sit in my truck, staring at the house I once called home. At first glance, it's all familiar—the long driveway, the wraparound porch, the way the trees sway like they're whispering secrets. But then it hits me like a punch in the gut—the decay.

Paint is peeling like old scabs, shutters hanging crooked like they've given up trying, and ivy is climbing the walls like it's claiming what's left. It's not just wear and tear—it's neglect. It's time. It's the past left to rot.

I step out of my truck, the crunch of gravel under my boots grounding me as I straighten my back. Old habits die hard. My muscles coil, ready for anything, like I'm walking into a war zone instead of my family's front yard. SEAL life doesn't just leave you—it's branded into your bones. There's no off switch for that, not even here. Not even now.

The home is over one hundred years old, but this depreciation isn't just about weather or time. Nah, the scars on this place run deeper than that.

It's like the building has been through its own battles while I was gone. My father loved this place's heritage and traditions, but he was a terrible businessman, and it shows.

I close my eyes and taste the hint of salt in the air from the nearby ocean. The distant sound of birds chirping and the low hum of cicadas rustle with the breeze, and I take a deep, calming breath. I only open my eyes when I hear the familiar creak of the mansion's front door opening and closing.

There—my mother, Ann Gloria Freeman, stands framed in the doorway like the queen she is. It's common knowledge that my mother is a beautiful woman. She's the poster child for the adage that Black don't crack, because even at seventy, she doesn't look a day over forty. The copper skin she inherited from her Piscataway Native American blood is smooth and unlined. At the same time, her gray hair looks platinum piled above her high cheekbones in her signature loose bun. Her face is highlighted by the sparkling hazel eyes that I share. As I step closer, I notice her eyes welling like the bay after a storm, and I push my six-foot-five frame up the eight steps separating us and run into her arms. The hug that envelops me is as warm as the summer air, thick with magnolia scent and recent sorrows.

"Jabari," she breathes, her voice cracking like the old oak by the chapel. "It's been too long, son."

"Mama." I exhale before my gaze lands on the wreath behind her—a circle of magnolias and black roses hanging like a shadow over the entrance. *Sorry, Dad. Love you.* Words left unsaid enter my thoughts. They're now orphaned by time and distance. A single tear betrays me, slipping free without permission.

I should have come back sooner.

I gently pull away from the suffocating comfort of my mother's arms. "Are any of my brothers here yet?" I ask, clearing my throat and shifting the weight of emotions onto practical concern. We all left home and started lives elsewhere after we graduated from Morehouse College, but I'm the only one who stayed away. At least they visit.

"They're coming in later this afternoon," she replies with a knowing smile. I've never been comfortable with big emotions. Ma used to joke that I never cried as a baby; I only scowled in displeasure. She dabs at her eyes with a tissue before straightening the silk wrap covering her shoulders.

Ma steps back, holding the door open wide, and I cross the threshold, feeling both welcome and like a stranger in the house I grew up in. The room's warmth wraps around me, the faint scent of lavender and something faintly sweet—her signature candle, always burning.

"Sit, Jabari." She motions to the sofa, which hasn't changed since I was a kid. The cushions are a little more worn now; the fabric faded in places, but it still feels like home.

I sink into the seat, but the weight of the space presses down on me, and I know I need to say it—the words I've been holding back for too long.

"I'm sorry," I start, my voice low and rough. I glance down at my hands, unsure how to meet her gaze. "For staying away. For not being here. I should've come home more. I should've—"

She cuts me off with a wave of her hand, her soft smile lined with understanding and sadness. "You had your reasons, Jabari. And I know your father... he knew them too."

"But I left you to handle everything," I press, the guilt rising in my throat. "The house, the business, him. You shouldn't have had to do it alone."

She reaches for my hand, her fingers cool but steady as they curl around mine. "Jabari, you've been carrying the weight of this family in your way, even from afar. Your father knew how much you sacrificed. And he was proud of you—so proud."

The words hit me square in the chest, loosening something I didn't realize was so tightly wound. I shake my head, still fighting the regret. "I didn't do enough. But I promise you, Ma—things will be different now. I'll take care of you.

Now that he's gone, I'll ensure you have everything you need."

Her eyes shimmer, a soft smile breaking through her grief. "Oh, baby," she says, her voice like honey. "You've always taken care of us. Don't you know that? Your father saw it. I see it. But what I need more than anything is you here. Not just fixing things, not just solving problems. I need my son."

The knot in my chest both tightens and loosens; her words feel simultaneously heavy and liberating.

"I'm here," I tell her, my voice steady now. "For a long while this time. I'll make sure you're never alone."

She squeezes my hand, her smile soft but full of something I haven't seen in a while—hope. "That sounds good to me, Jabari."

As we sit there, the silence stretching between us like a comforting quilt, I realize this moment, this promise, is the start of something new—a chance to rebuild, heal, and finally come home.

* * *

"Are you hungry, Bari?" My mother's question is soft, but I catch the undercurrent of normality she is trying to weave into the fabric of this distorted day.

I've been home for forty-eight hours now, helping my mother prepare for my father's funeral services, and my siblings have avoided me. There's a lot of healing that must happen between us, but I'm hoping that I at least see my baby sister, Amara, today. My brothers resent me for leaving, and I resent them for feeling that way.

My mother has coddled me the entire time I've been here, and I must admit I miss the care. I stay to myself in VA Beach, and no one fusses over me.

"I'm always hungry," I say, forcing a smile, willing my stomach to agree. Truth is, I've been in a perpetual state of nausea since she called me two days ago to say that Papa had passed. The man who held us all together, even from a distance, is gone. It was unexpected and rocked me to my core.

"Then let's go to the clubhouse and get you fed. You can see Marty. She's been asking about you."

I roll my eyes but smile. Marty, or Martha Jenkins, is my mother's best friend, godmother, and the town's busybody. She manages the Chesapeake Heights Country Club with an Iron fist swathed in a lace glove for my family. She's a living relic of Southern hospitality with a side of sass that could slice through steel. I'm not in the mood for a visit right now, but that doesn't matter. For my mother's sake, I agree, "Yes, ma'am."

She laughs at my formality; her chuckle is a sound that could soothe the most savage storms—storms that this old place has seen too many of. She pulls back, hands gripping my arms as if anchoring me to the here and now, to the reality of home and all the complications the word carries.

"You always were too serious for your own good," she says, her gaze scanning my face like she's searching for the boy she raised beneath the furrowed brow of the man I've become.

"Serious keeps you alive," I reply, but the smirk makes a comeback. "You taught me that."

"Did I, now?" she asks, arching an eyebrow. "Or did I teach you that family keeps you alive?"

I want to scoff, to tell her that she's wrong, but the truth of her words settles heavily in my gut. I glance past her shoulder, taking in the sagging roofline, the garden that's more weed than bloom, and the echoes of laughter that used to bounce off these walls.

"Let's walk," I suggest because standing still feels too much like sinking.

"Lead the way, son," she says, and there's pride in her voice, laced with steel; it tells me we're not going to reminisce about the good old days during this walk and lunch. We've got battles to face, debts to settle, and a legacy to uphold.

This resort—it's more than just land and buildings. It's the blood and sweat of generations, and as much as I might want to run from it all to avoid the messiness of what's been left behind, I know there's no outrunning family. Not really.

"Still standing, ain't it?" I say, gesturing vaguely at the expanse of the resort as we pass various buildings.

"Always," she affirms, her smile unwavering as we enter the fray of the bustling resort. "But much has changed," she starts, and I can hear the burden of what she is carrying in her voice.

I nod. "Dad used to say that change is the only constant," I reply, my gaze taking in the tattered but usable tennis courts and the warping windows of the main hall. It's like seeing a family portrait where everyone's aged, but you remember them young.

Mom glances at me, her eyes sharp, knowing. "Ten years is a long time to be gone, Jabari. I know everything looks older to you, but it can be brought back to glory. We just got to have a little faith."

I feel the weight of her gaze, the expectation. My mind spins, calculations firing off like rounds in a chamber. The cost of repairs and unpaid bills stack up like bricks in a wall too high to climb. Can we breathe life into this place again, or should we write a eulogy alongside my father's for a dream long dead?

"Faith doesn't pay the bills, Mama." I can't keep the bitterness from my voice; the taste of it is as familiar as blood. Faith sure as hell didn't keep my fiancée chaste while I was halfway across the world, dodging bullets.

"Money isn't everything. We've survived on less," she counters, her chin lifting defiantly.

I know then to say no more. She's not ready to hear it.

We walk side by side, her arm looped through mine as though we're soldiers marching in unspoken solidarity against whatever the world throws at us. We take the easiest route to the clubhouse alongside the beach at the back of our home. For a few moments, we move in silence, the rhythmic crash of the waves a constant companion, their deep roar a soothing balm against the weight of the past.

But as we near the resort's clubhouse, a familiar spark lights in her eyes. Her shoulders straighten, and a small smile plays at the corner of her lips. "Jabari," she begins, her voice both weary and resolute, "things have been tough the past few years. We've held it together by threads of prayer but with your father gone... I don't know what we'll do. But I know this—having you here with us will make all the difference. Everything will be all right because Chesapeake Heights is your destiny."

She pats my back with a tenderness that only she can give, and that smile is the kind that could make anyone believe in miracles.

The weight of her words settles on my shoulders, an invisible yoke crafted from loss and legacy.

The summer breeze whips against my face, and the winds of change are at my heels. My father has died, and I can't shake the feeling that something or someone is coming to shake us up in his wake.

I've only been in Chesapeake Heights for an hour, and control, that elusive beast, seems to be slipping through my fingers like the sands on the beach where I played as a child. And with each step toward the clubhouse, toward Marty, and her inevitable barrage of questions, I brace myself for what's to come.

TWO

Too Late to Turn Back Now

SIERRA

MY PHONE BUZZES ON THE PASSENGER SEAT, AND I hit the speaker button without taking my eyes off the winding road ahead. My best friend Tiana's voice cuts through the silence, sharp and full of annoyance.

"Where are you?" she snaps, skipping the pleasantries. "You were supposed to call me back hours ago."

"I'm driving," I reply, my tone light. "Heading out to Calvert County for a job interview at Chesapeake Heights Resort. And Girl! Now I get why Dorothy told Toto she wasn't in Kansas anymore," I grumble as I glance at the miles of trees stretching endlessly before me. "This place is *far*."

And that's the truth. For the past forty-five minutes, I've been driving down Route 4, watching the gritty streets of DC and the busy highways of PG County transform into the lush, tree-lined calm of Calvert County. It feels like stepping into another world where time slows down, and the weight of city life fades with every mile.

I've been a proud Washingtonian for twenty-six years, navigating the Beltway like a pro and never venturing far from its loops and turns. Sure, I've driven down Pennsylvania Avenue plenty of times, but not all the way down. I didn't even realize Pennsylvania Avenue turns into Route 4.

I've been as far as Upper Marlboro—Show Place Arena for my high school graduation, thank you very much. But beyond that? It's not my scene. Everyone in my community knows the unspoken rules about Chesapeake Beach, that tucked-away corner of Calvert County where the air feels heavier for folks like me.

"Why are you hauling your hard-headed behind way out there? There are plenty of summer jobs in DC!" Tiana hollers through my car's Bluetooth, her tone dripping with self-righteousness.

"Yes, Tiana, I know there are plenty of summer jobs in DC," I snap, rolling my eyes even though she can't see me. "But none of them pay *this* much."

She's quiet for a beat before scoffing. "Hold up. Why are you even working during your summer off? Isn't that the whole point of becoming a *school* psychologist?"

I hesitate. She knows me too well. "Oh, I just wanted some extra cash to cushion the rest of the year," I lie, trying to sound convincing.

"Unh-unh," she says, her voice narrowing. "This is about Shana, isn't it? What's she done now?"

See, this is why I didn't want to tell her.

I grip the steering wheel tighter, my knuckles tightening. "Listen, Tiana. She's in trouble. Real trouble."

"She's *always* in trouble, Sierra. Be specific."

"She owes money," I say, my voice barely above a whisper

like saying it out loud might make it worse. "A lot of it. To Dominion."

Tiana inhales sharply, and I can practically feel her disbelief through the line. "Dominion? As in Jackson Taylor and his merry band of psychopaths? Tell me you're joking."

"I wish I were," I mutter, my chest tightening. "She's been gambling again. She thought she could win enough to pay off her other debts, but now she's in over her head."

My sister's gambling debts are out of control. And this time, if we don't come up with the cash she owes, Shana's life might be on the line, and mine by association.

"Damn it, Sierra!" Tiana's frustration crackles through the line. "How much?"

"Twenty-five grand."

The line goes silent momentarily, and then Tiana's voice comes back, low and laced with fear. "Sierra, you need to stay the hell out of this. Do you hear me? You know what Jackson's capable of. You're not some action hero. Let her deal with her own mess for once."

"Tiana, Shana took me in when Mama died. I was sixteen and she was only twenty-one. She sacrificed too much for me; I can't just throw her away." I snap, my voice breaking. "She's scared. They're threatening her. And if they can't get to her, they'll come for me. I can't just sit back and do nothing."

"And what exactly do you think you're going to do? Write them a check?" Tiana's sarcasm is biting, but I can hear the concern underneath it. "You don't have that kind of money, Sierra. You're barely keeping yourself afloat as it is."

"I don't have it yet," I admit, my grip tightening on the wheel. "But, this job at Chesapeake Heights pays twenty-five hundred dollars[Paula Gru1] a week. I have to try. She's my sister, Tiana. If something happens to her…"

Tiana exhales, her anger softening into something more

protective. "Listen to me. Jackson Taylor isn't someone you mess with. You can't just march into Chesapeake Heights and hope for the best. You need a plan. You need backup. What if you don't get the job?"

"I don't have time for a plan," I say, my voice trembling despite my best effort to stay calm. "They gave her four weeks, Tiana. And knowing Jackson, that's a generous deadline."

"Four weeks?" she echoes, the fear now evident in her tone. "Sierra, this is insane. You need to get out of town. Now."

"I can't," I say firmly. "I won't abandon her."

The line goes quiet again, and when Tiana speaks, her voice is softer, resigned. "Just... be careful, okay? I don't want to get a call saying they found you in a ditch somewhere."

"I will," I promise, though the weight in my chest tells me it's a lie. This is a storm I can't outrun, no matter how hard I try.

"And watch your speed," she commands. "You know you don't want to get pulled over out there. Calvert County is not for us."

I laugh despite myself. "Tiana Mitchell, you do know that Black people live out here too, right?"

She lets out a dramatic *spshhh,* the sound dripping with skepticism. "It can't be that many. And how do you know that? I've never heard you mention Calvert County before. Like, ever."

I roll my eyes, though her curiosity tugs at a corner of my memory I don't visit often.

"Have you forgotten that I went to college with some of the bougiest Black people in America? Howard isn't called the Black Mecca for no reason, Tiana. Trust me, it's a hub for generational Black wealth and an even tighter network of upward mobility."

"Yes, Ms. Bison," Tiana exhales. I don't need to see Tiana's face to know she's smirking. I can hear it in her voice. "I know where you went to school. And I know that that network never invited your poor, orphaned behind into their little circle."

"Whatever," I shoot back, rolling my eyes. "Just because I wasn't part of their clique doesn't mean I didn't know what they were up to. Many of their families—especially the DMV and East Coast crowd—summered in Chesapeake Heights. They've got houses there."

"And let me guess," she says, her voice dripping with sarcasm, "your ex-boyfriend's family was one of them? What happened? You never got an invite because he didn't want Mommy and Daddy Dearest to know you existed?"

Ouch. That truth hurt.

"Tiana, that was mean," I snap, but my voice comes out softer than I want. "I thought you were working on not saying everything that pops into your head. That hurt my feelings."

She exhales, the sigh heavy with guilt. "I'm sorry, girl. Really, I am. I just worry about you. You know I couldn't stand Thomas's stuck-up ass. He treated you like *he* was the prize throughout college, like you were supposed to feel grateful just because his family had money."

Her words cut deeper because they're true. She doesn't stop.

"I remember every time his family went to their fancy 'summer house,' and you'd make excuses about why you couldn't go. Said you had to work. But we both know the truth. He never invited you. Never wanted you there. And I just... I don't want to see you chasing ghosts from your past."

Her words dig deep, unearthing memories I'd rather leave buried. She's right; I always made excuses for Thomas' behavior, and she always saw right through it.

Tiana's voice softens, but it still carries the edge of a protective big sister. "His family may have been rich, but they were terrible people for what they did to you. Sometimes, I wish you'd just gone to Wilson High School and the University of Maryland with me. At least the prejudiced White folks there showed their hand. Our people are sneaky with it."

I close my eyes as the memory hits me, fresh and sharp. Graduation day. The end of six years with Thomas. Six years of being his queen 80 percent of the time and feeling like a charity case the other 20 percent. We met at Maret Prep School when I was a sophomore. I was the scholarship student, and he was the heir to the third defense contracting firm[Paula Gru2] in DC. He was manipulative, toxic, entitled, and mean when he wanted to be—but I thought we were forever. Because for so long, we were.

Until we weren't.

When his rich mama and daddy told him it was time to get serious and that he needed to find "marriage material" before starting Harvard Law, he dropped me like yesterday's news. I guess a big booty girl from Anacostia wasn't what they had in mind for their son.

That's the heart of it for Tiana. She's not trying to be a bitch, she just never got over the way Thomas discarded me for being poor, and if I'm being honest, neither have I.

She let me crash at her apartment for months after Thomas ended things. We shared an expensive apartment in Southwest DC on the Wharf, and when he moved out, I could not afford the rent.

Tiana had warned me about getting an apartment with him that I could not afford. She said you n*ever put your living arrangements in a man's hands,* but I didn't listen. When I showed up on her doorstep, distraught, she didn't say, "I told you so." Instead, she dried my tears while we watched reruns of *Girlfriends* and shared endless cartons of rocky road ice cream.

"I know you love me, girl," I say, my voice steady now. "And

I'll be fine. I promise I'm not chasing ghosts, and I'm not about to let anyone from my past mess with my head. Chesapeake Heights is about work, not drama."

Tiana is quiet for a moment, and when she speaks, her voice is warm, the sharp edges smoothed by love. "All right, then. But be careful. You hear me? Love you!"

"Love you too," I reply, a smile tugging at my lips despite myself.

As I hang up, I take a deep breath, steadying myself. This is a new chapter, a new chance.

Chesapeake Heights is one of the wealthiest Black summer communities in the country. The beach club is practically legendary, and the Activities Director position I'm interviewing for pays as much as my school psychologist salary. That's the kind of money that could save Shana's life and buy me some peace of mind. And that's the only reason I'm going.

I glance at the GPS as the road ahead narrows, flanked by pristine trees swaying in the summer breeze. I'm praying the uppity people of this community will look past my big auburn afro, nose ring, and wine-red lips and give me a chance. I refuse to pretend to be someone I'm not just to get a job. There's no hiding my curves. I've got what the old folks call birthing hips and ass for days. They are getting all this body, and today. *But they had better know that this body comes with brains.*

My phone interview with the resort's owner and executive director, Ann Freeman, was terrific. I got formal but friendly vibes from her. We talked about my love of Black History and how I'd love to intertwine the resort's history into some activities for the guests. She was impressed and told me to dress casually for the interview. Well, she's getting this yellow wrap dress, and hopefully, my double D's won't peek out the top since I pinned them down, but that's the best I can do.

I swear this is my third and final time bailing my sister out. I don't generally give anyone a chance to make a fool of me twice, and my failed relationship taught me that.

But my sister is my weakness. She's made playing in my face a sport.

We never knew our father, and Shana saved me from the horrors of foster care and group homes when Mama died. I feel like I owe her, but even I have my limits. She needs help, and me handing her money to dig herself deeper isn't the answer.

Today is also the tenth anniversary of our mother's death, and the pain is still raw. You never really get over the death of a parent, and I woke up today weighed down by sadness and grief. Our mother was everything to us, and since she's been gone, I haven't been the same. I want to finish this interview and head home to a pan of mac and cheese, a pint of Caramel Core Ben and Jerry's Ice Cream, and a bottle of Riesling wine.

I slow as I turn off the main boardwalk and onto Whistling Pines Avenue, and the Chesapeake Heights Beach Resort gates come into view. They're massive, an imposing structure probably used to intimidate as much as impress. I stop at a security station to be let through.

The heavyset security guard, a woman with a scowl carved deep into her face, glares at me from her post as I pull up to the gates of the Chesapeake Heights Beach Resort. She's wearing a black uniform that stretches slightly over her wide frame, her arms crossed tightly in front of her chest, and an attitude that matches her no-nonsense posture. She doesn't bother to hide her annoyance when I roll down my window.

"Where's your code?" she demands, her voice sharp and dismissive, the words spat out like I'm already guilty of some unspoken crime.

I straighten in my seat, my irritation spiking at her tone. "I've got it," I reply, forcing calm into my voice despite the rush of heat under my skin.

I dig through my purse, my fingers brushing against the random chaos of receipts, Dior lip gloss, and pens, but no code. Of course. My heart kicks into overdrive, and I can feel her judgment-heavy gaze burning through me.

"Typical," she mutters, low enough that I almost don't catch it. "Outsiders always causing trouble."

My jaw tightens. Oh no, she did not just— I flick my eyes back to her, lifting a brow. "Excuse me?" I shoot back, a slight smirk tugging at the corner of my lips. "Do you have a problem with me, or is this just your personality?"

She raises an eyebrow, clearly not expecting the comeback. I dig deeper into my bag, pretending to ignore the growing frustration. My fingers finally graze the scrap of paper I scribbled the code on, but my relief is short-lived as I realize it's still a mess of numbers and symbols that's hard to read.

Damn, my messy handwriting.

Just now, I checked my phone for a backup. As I scroll through my notes, I find it—the code is finally clear and ready. Without missing a beat, I hold up the phone to her.

"Here. Now, do your job," I add, the challenge in my voice unmistakable.

I see a flicker of fight in her eyes, but she quickly masks it. *Good, because she doesn't want this smoke.* She grunts something unintelligible under her breath before reluctantly waving me through.

The gravel crunches under the tires of my ten-year-old Camry as I finally approach the grand estate where the main offices are located. It's a sprawling white mansion with intricate details and towering columns, surrounded by lush, manicured gardens spread out for miles. I can even see the beauty of the bay behind it.

I park behind a giant black truck and stare at the beautiful old home, my breath catching. It's like something out of a Black fairy tale, where wealthy families come to hide away from the rest of the world.

This is the place, Baycrest.

I grip the door handle, the weight of this interview hitting me hard. I feel a shiver run down my spine as I step out of the car, my feet sinking into the plush grass. This is it. No turning back now. I breathe deeply, smooth my dress, and step onto the perfectly manicured lawn.

Hell, even their grass is luxurious.

Where I grew up, our definition of luxury was a night uninterrupted by gunshots. The peace I feel just being on this property sets me ill at ease. Peace is not something I'm used to.

As I walk toward the entrance, my heels sinking into the soft grass, I can feel the weight of everything that's come before me with every step. This place, this resort, was built by the sweat and dreams of people like me—the Black elite who fought for their slice of paradise in a world that tried to keep them out.

But there's something else hanging in the air, too—a quiet sense of entitlement, like the folks here think they've earned everything just because they were born into it. I can feel it as I approach the big double doors, like they're ready to slam shut before I even get through. Like they expect me to apologize just for showing up.

But that's not happening. Not now. Not ever.

"May I help you?" A beautiful young woman with a fierce stare and an even fiercer running outfit pauses at the bottom of the steps to size me up. Her stare is wary but not unfriendly. "Do you have an appointment at Baycrest this afternoon?"

I nod and find my voice. "Yes, I'm Sierra Watson, and I'm interviewing for the summer activities director position with Ms. Ann Freeman. Do you know where I can find her?"

She looks at me thoughtfully before smirking. "Ms. Ann is unavailable, but her son Jabari Freeman is covering for her. I think I saw him heading into the Clubhouse not too long ago. Wait here, and I'll get him." She gives me one more glance before saying," Good luck."

My spidey senses tingle. "WAIT, what does that mean—"

She doesn't wait. Instead, she runs off behind the house and toward the beach to get this Jabari she speaks of. I sigh, knowing that this interview is already going south. I have a feeling from the smirk she gave and the comment she made that Jabari is a piece of work. And I don't have time for any man's shenanigans today. I've got to get this job. I'm out of other options, so I head downstairs and wait.

But no matter how frustrated I get, I can't just walk away. I can't let anyone hurt my sister. Shana is all I have left, and I refuse to throw her to the wolves.

THREE

Take the Long Way Home

JABARI

When I walk into the clubhouse, the first thing that hits me is the familiar scent of fried crab cakes mixed with old money. The atmosphere is alive with activity: members talking at the bar, families enjoying meals in the restaurant, and staff bustling about like busy bees.

"Hey Jabari!" Marty calls out from behind her podium. She's a petite woman with big hair and an even bigger personality. Her face lights up when she sees me.

"Hi, Marty," I say, giving her a brief hug. "How's everything going?"

"Oh, you know, busy as always," she replies with a wink. "But it's good to have you back. I'll be over to join y'all in a minute."

"It's good to be back," I say, though I'm unsure if that's true. My mother takes me to a table in a quiet corner of the restaurant. We sit down, order our food, and engage in small talk.

"So, how have things been since last summer's storm?" I ask, trying to steer the conversation back toward more practical matters.

My mother sighs and looks down at her hands before meeting my gaze again. "It's been tough," she says softly. "Many of our older cottages were destroyed or damaged beyond repair. Plus, numerous people in town lost their businesses, too." I nod, knowing all too well about the devastation caused by Hurricane Isolde. Our family was fortunate enough only to suffer minimal damage to Baycrest and our main businesses, but many in town weren't so lucky.

"I've been working closely with Mayor Wilkins to help with relief efforts," she continues. "And your brothers have also been lending a hand whenever possible."

"That's great," I respond, proud of my family for stepping up during such a tough time. Still, I can't shake the guilt of not being here to help.

"Several developers are hovering around our property like vultures, but I won't allow them to take even an inch of our family's land. I'll defend our legacy until the bitter end. You know your father would've done the same if he were still with us," my mother says with a touch of nostalgia.

I grasp her hand, providing a bit of solace. We both understand that my father's absence will deeply affect our family, and she clearly anticipates that I should take on his role. She hopes I will advocate for a legacy I abandoned a decade ago, but I suspect she might be the only one with faith in my ability.

Marty's arrival and a waitress trailing behind her break the solemnity. Marty quickly slides into the booth next to me.

"Jabari Freeman, look at you!" She smacks her lips after planting a wet kiss on my cheek. "Been too long, boy."

"Ms. Martha," I nod, acknowledging the elephant-sized gap of years and miles between us.

"Crabcake sandwich, fries, and a corona," I tell the waitress, an order I know by heart despite the years. Ma orders a wedge salad, light on the blue cheese, and Marty? Wine, as if it were an extension of herself. Once the waitress leaves, she lays into me.

"Vanessa was in town with her and Jason's new baby last week," Marty says, twisting the knife without blinking." I saw her in Target shopping for the baby with that criminal brother of hers, Jackson. She asked about you, but you know I acted like I didn't hear a word she said. Yep, I sure did... I ignored her real good. What did you ever see in that trashy girl, nephew? I told you she was a ho."

Here we go...

"Marty!" Ma's voice rises in a half-hearted protest. "You know goodness well that Jabari doesn't want to hear anything about that trashy Vee Taylor and that wretched boy she married. And watch your mouth!"

"Exactly," I mutter, clenching my jaw. "She's yesterday's mistake."

I spent a considerable amount of time on elite missions around the globe to finally move on from my cheating ex-fiancée. I'm a man who has always lived by a code of integrity and loyalty, so it was difficult to comprehend how the two people I loved most, apart from my family, could turn my trust into a loaded weapon, obliterating my heart.

It's been ten years since I've seen them, and that is by design. Partly because I'm still not sure, I won't put a bullet in Jason's reckless ass on sight. Mostly because I don't like the emotions that stir when facing what they did, I'd instead block that entire part of my life out. Those two are why I keep my distance from people and Chesapeake Heights.

Ms. Marty claps her hands." I'm glad to hear that because

it's time for you to marry and move on." I open my mouth to tell her I have moved on, but she raises a hand and shushes me. "It's time to give your poor mother some grandbabies. Shame your daddy never got to hold one," she continues, blissfully ignorant of the razor-edged words she flung around.

I gulp my beer in record time while Marty and my mother bicker, fuss, and then laugh over me.

"Excuse me," I grunt, suddenly finding my appetite waning under the weight of her judgments. "I want to check on the horses at the barn before everyone arrives. "Standing up, I kiss both women on their foreheads and ignore their stunned looks. Then, I leave out the back door to escape the conditioned air for the caress of summer's sea breeze.

"Sneaking back to Virginia already, brother?" A voice calls out, and I smile at the only woman besides my mother who brings me joy: my baby sister Amara.

Amara's face shines with mischief as she approaches me quietly from behind. When she grins, she has our mother's sparkling hazel eyes and a dimple on her left cheek. On this lovely summer day, she's wearing a carefree sundress, the sky's hue.

I wrap her in a bear hug until she squeals for mercy. "Of course not. You know I'd never leave without hugging my favorite girl. How are you doing, Little bit?"

She rolls her eyes at the nickname I've had for her since she was born. Amara is ten years younger than me and has always felt like my baby in many ways. Even though she's twenty-five now, she's still Littlebit to me. "I wish you would stop calling me that, and don't pretend like you haven't snuck out of town on me before. I'm pretty sure that if Daddy hadn't died this morning, you'd be on your way back to Virginia by sundown.

I hate that what she's saying is true, but I can't deny it.

"Well, I'll be around for a while this time. Mama wants me

to stick around and help with some of the resort's operations and finances now that Papa—"

I can't even say he's gone. It's just unreal. My sister understands and nods. "I was just having lunch with her and Marty."

Amara laughs. "Let me guess, Ms. Marty started talking crazy, and you got out of there before you said something disrespectful."

I chuckle. "Yep, you've got it."

Amara sighs. "Well, I'm going inside now for my dose of, "Girl, when will you get married and give your mama some grandbabies? Being a lawyer ain't gonna keep them curves warm at night." We snicker and make fake gagging noises at her Marty impression before she continues, "Mama called me down here, and I couldn't tell her no."

But look, if you'll be here for a while, get your mind right for Malik. Our brother is definitely on one lately. That Hotep shit has gotten out of control, and you know he's always resented you for leaving and not coming back. He thinks he's in charge now as the second-born, even though he's only been dropping in from New York once a month to boss Mama and Daddy around. Be prepared for the foolishness."

I nod. "I figured as much. Don't worry, I know how to handle his irresponsible ass. What about Asa and Amir?" I ask about my two younger brothers, curious how they feel about me and their place at the resort. I know they often visit the resort, coming for all the major holidays, but they still keep their distance.

Amara shrugs. "They're cool, you know, the twins—they keep their own thing going on in LA. They're still secretive and sneaky as shit, but they're harmless." She stands on her tiptoes and kisses me on my cheek goodbye before I can inquire what she's up to. "Gotta go, bro. Can't keep Mama waiting."

I let her scurry off and make a mental note to find out what or who she's been into lately. But right now, I need a quiet walk on the beach.

Reaching the sand feels like the rough embrace of old, abrasive, and warm memories. I became a man on these shores, not the soil of foreign land soaked in blood. Marching in the army of the Freeman legacy was all the boot camp any of my brothers needed to grow from boys to men.

The men went to Morehouse in the Freeman Family, and the girls went to Spelman. So, top grades in high school were a must. My great-grandfather, Robert Freeman, graduated from Morehouse in 1919 before promptly being drafted by the US Navy as a second lieutenant. After he served his time for Uncle Sam, he bought the land that is now Chesapeake Heights in 1920 and developed it. He started by building our family home, Baycrest.

My grandfather, Michael Freeman, followed in his footsteps, leaving Morehouse in 1951 with a degree in architecture and design and joining the Korean War fight in the Navy. When he returned, he built up most of what we know as Chesapeake Heights today.

Our father, Marcus Freeman, joined Morehouse's Navy ROTC program and graduated in 1979. He never served in a war, but he served his four years as a commissioned officer just the same.

Our paths were set when my brothers and I came along. We graduated from Morehouse and joined the Navy ROTC program, except for Malik. However, after graduation, I applied and was selected for the Navy SEAL program and Team Six. I was only twenty-one and brimming with bravado. I had never really fit in anywhere; I'm quiet and broody. I'm also big, so people always kept their distance once I reached middle school. Everyone, except for Vee and Jason—they understood me.

That's why I asked her to marry me one day after church as soon as I received my Morehouse degree.

After serving four years, I always planned to return and serve the family business, just as my father did before me. But when one mission turned into three. I had my doubts. I loved what I was doing but wasn't sure if I wanted to come home and run a resort.

I kept Vee hanging on to a diamond ring and a promise for three years; I can't blame her for getting tired. But I can blame her for being dishonest, and I certainly can blame my former best friend for sleeping with my fiancée.

I'm fuming over the past and deep in my thoughts when I see Raven Ambrose, my younger brother Asa's secret love and thorn in my side, biking my way.

Our family has been at odds over land with the Ambrose family for as long as I can remember, but it never stopped those two from screwing like rabbits whenever they could find a corner to hide in. Then they would come out of the dark fighting like they couldn't stand the sight of each other in public. The secrecy was all Raven's idea because she feared what her father and four brothers would think. I never understood why Asa put up with her bullshit. My brother is too good of a dude to be hidden away.

But what do I know? I was engaged to my first love, and I still got burned. Maybe falling for an obvious enemy is the way to go.

As usual, Raven's wearing defiance like a second skin. Surprisingly she stops right in front of me.

"Jabari," she says, her voice clipped, sharp—a note of feigned sympathy that never quite reaches her eyes. She's never forgiven me for trying to keep her and Asa apart and whooping her slimy brother Sean's tail twice when he tried to come for me in high school. I can feel that old bitterness simmering beneath the surface when she speaks. "Sorry about Mr. Freeman. *He* was a good man."

She places an almost imperceptible emphasis on the word *he*, as though she's reminding me that I don't quite measure up. The sting is subtle but sharp. Sadly, she may be right, and the truth bites deeper than I want to admit.

"Thanks," I reply curtly, my words tight, unwilling to give her any more than she's already gotten. I won't unravel in front of her, not now.

"How long are you staying around to help your mom?" It's an innocent enough question on the surface, but I can feel the judgment curling beneath it, probing at the walls I've built.

"I'm not sure yet," I reply, my words sharp. "I've got a life, an important Naval career back in VA Beach." The gruffness in my tone is a shield, one I raise high against her relentless scrutiny. "But my mom knows she can always call me if needed. I'm only a few hours away."

Her eyes narrow slightly, but her voice remains as unfazed as ever. "Could've fooled me," she replies, a hint of amusement lacing her words. "We haven't seen you in nearly ten years." She allows the silence to linger, heavy with years of unspoken words. "Since you're here to help, you can start by greeting the woman waiting in front of your house. She said her name is Sierra Watson, and she's here to interview for the summer activities director position. Your mom probably never got the chance to call and cancel with everything going on."

"Great," I mutter, my sarcasm dripping like venom. Raven throws me a look—a dare, almost. Her eyes glint with the knowing that dares me to rise to it. With a grunt, I jog away, counting the seconds until this unexpected responsibility is over.

When I reach the front of the house, I'm already bracing myself to deal with the inevitable awkwardness of canceling an interview day. I'm prepared to cut through the pleasantries and dismiss the applicant quickly.

Then, I see her.

I can only see her in profile, but that silhouette is enough to make me stumble.

She waits for me like a beautiful challenge I should resist. The stunning woman stands poised and confident, exuding an aura that resembles a quiet storm.

I take a deep breath and calm my beating heart—because something tells me this encounter won't be as simple as I thought.

FOUR

Goodbye Girl

SIERRA

I'VE BEEN WAITING TWENTY MINUTES FOR JABARI Freeman—or whoever is meant to interview me—twenty *long* minutes. My patience is wearing thin, just like my bank account, and my frustration is bubbling dangerously close to the surface. Tardiness embodies arrogance. If you can't respect my time, why should I respect you? But this job is my only option, so I'll sit here and swallow my pride, no matter how bitter it is.

I lean against the iron fence, trying to steady my breathing. The lavish posts likely_cost more than my rent for a year—the decorative balustrades feel oppressive, as if mocking me. The harder I try to focus, the louder Shana's voice echoes in my head:

"Sierra, I need help. Jackson's gonna kill me. Please, I'm scared."

The desperation in her words still haunts me, twisting my

stomach into knots. Jackson Taylor. The name alone sends a chill down my spine. He's not just Shana's dangerous ex-boyfriend—he's the heir to *Dominion,* the crime family that rules the DMV like a kingdom. He's the one who introduced her to his gambling dens, all seductive charm and toxic promises. She thought he was exciting. I saw a snake in a designer suit.

And now, thanks to him, my sister owes twenty-five thousand dollars to people who make their living collecting on debts. The kind of people who don't accept IOUs or second chances. Shana says she can't pay it. She swears she's trying to get her life together. But I've heard this story before. She cries. She promises. And I'm always the one left scrambling to clean up her mess.

Still, she's my sister. My *only* family. I've already lost too much and won't lose her too—not to Jackson Taylor or Dominion.

My phone buzzes, jolting me out of my spiraling thoughts. The number on the screen is one I wish I could ignore. My chest tightens, but I answer anyway.

"Well, well," Jackson's voice oozes through the line, smooth and venomous. "I wondered when I'd hear from the *other* Watson sister."

"What do you want, Jackson?" My voice is sharp, but my hands are trembling.

"Four weeks, Sierra," he says, his tone dripping with mock patience. "Four weeks to come up with twenty-five large. I'd hate for anything to happen to that sexy little ass of yours. Dominion doesn't forgive a debt."

"Leave me out of this. Shana—"

"Shana's mistakes are your problem now. Family first, right?" He laughs, low and cruel, and I grip the phone tighter to keep from flinging it across the room. "Don't test me, Sierra. I'll be watching. I hope you can't pay because then maybe you and I can work something "personal" out to work out your sister's debt.

The call ends before I can respond, leaving me frozen, my breath caught in my chest. The world feels smaller as if the sky is pressing down and the earth is pushing up. My heart races, and panic claws at my throat. I wipe my damp palms against my skirt, trying to maintain my composure, but fear has already seeped into every corner of me.

I'm startled when a deep, commanding voice cuts through my anxious stream of consciousness.

"Can I help you?"

I jump, my heart racing. A tall, imposing man with undeniable authority appears to have materialized from thin air. His presence is dominating, and his gaze is sharp and intense. My pulse quickens, and I instinctively step back to regain my composure.

His dark skin gleams in the sunlight, making his sharp cheekbones and the strong line of his jaw look carved from stone. His beard, perfectly groomed, only enhances the sharpness of his features. Light but intense, his eyes hold something more than just a glance. It's like they're pulling me in, drawing me closer, trapping me in a world I know I shouldn't want to be part of. And the way he moves—graceful, fluid, like he's in control of everything around him—has my heart racing.

"I..." My voice falters, and I swallow hard, trying to gather myself. "I'm here for an interview."

He raises an eyebrow, his expression unreadable. "You must be Sierra Watson."

His voice clicks, but my mind is still spinning from the call. Jackson's voice lingers, a ghost that refuses to leave, and I can't stop my thoughts from racing. *Four weeks. Twenty-five thousand dollars. Pretty little ass.*

Jabari's sharp gaze narrows like he's reading the stress etched across my face. "Are you all right?"

No, I'm not. But I can't let him see that. Not yet. So, I plaster the most convincing smile I can muster and lie through my teeth.

He outstretches his hand as I stand there like a silent idiot. "I'm Jabari Freeman."

And that's when I smell him. His scent is faint but memorable—a heady mix of musk and sandalwood clings to him like a secret, an invitation to something wild and untamed. The kind of scent that makes you want to lose yourself in it.

But I can't afford to lose myself. Doing so could mean the end of my sister's life.

I shake my head and shake his hand quickly. "I—I'm here for an interview for the summer activities director position," I stammer, suddenly feeling small under his scrutiny. I hate feeling less than, and I decide I hate him for it.

I square my shoulders and try again. "I am scheduled to meet with Mrs. Ann Freeman," I say with a strong voice.

His hazel eyes flicker with recognition for a split second before a cool indifference settles over his face. He studies every inch of me, then speaks with a smooth tone laced with a hint of exasperation. "No, an interview with my mother is impossible today."

Impossible? His gruff words hit me like a slap. My mind spins, and I glance at my outfit, checking if I've missed the mark with my yellow wrap dress and gold-heeled sandals. I look like I belong here, don't I? Why would he dismiss me so quickly?

I feel the familiar fire of offense stir within me, and I refuse to let him brush me off like this. *Like Thomas did.* I had a great phone interview with his mother. That's who I need to speak with, not him. With a steadying breath, I lift my chin and meet his gaze, unwilling to let him see how rattled I am. "I had an excellent conversation with your mother, you know, the OWNER of this resort," I say, my voice firm. "I was promised an interview and resort tour with Mrs. Freeman, whom I intend to speak with. I'm not going anywhere until I do."

Jabari doesn't flinch at my words, and again, I hate how that somehow makes me shrink like I'm the one being unreasonable. His gaze narrows, calm and calculating, as if he's sizing me up, measuring the strength of my resolve. I can feel my pulse racing in my neck, and my skin feels too tight, like it's buzzing with something I can't quite identify.

"You're bold, I'll give you that," he says, his voice smooth, each word wrapped in a velvet-smooth edge. He's still leaning against the column at the bottom of the stairs, his body relaxed but radiating an energy so intense it's almost palpable. "But I don't hand out jobs for boldness. Not in this case. You'll need a proper interview, and no one can give you one." His eyes lock on mine, and I swear I can feel them burn through me.

I narrow my eyes, step forward, and challenge him. I'm a whole foot shorter than him, but I stand my ground and lift my chin a little higher. "I'm not asking for a handout," I say, my tone sharper now. "I've got skills and experience. I've got every-thing your mother wanted for this role, so she called me here. And I've traveled too far to be dismissed by her rude and enti-tled son."

He lifts an eyebrow at that, and the flicker of amusement returns, just enough to make me second-guess myself. "Oh, you've got something, all right, but your manners are lacking. Even if I did take the time to interview you, I don't think you know the first thing about the temperament and talent this job requires. After all, you would work directly under me."

I feel the heat rising in my cheeks, and I pray he doesn't see his last words' effect on me. Because God give me strength, but

I'd like to be under a body like his for hours; he looks like the kind of man who knows his way around the female anatomy.

I clear my throat and shake my head at the infatuation I'm experiencing, "You'd be surprised what I know," I reply coolly, crossing my arms again, this time to stop my hands from shaking. The motion draws his eyes to my bust, and I smirk at his weakness. "Besides, I'm a fast learner. More than capable of handling whatever you throw my way."

His lips curve slightly like a giant cat waiting to pounce on his food. "A fast learner, huh?" he murmurs, his voice low and teasing. "And what makes you think I'm the type of man who'll teach?"

I blink, momentarily caught off guard by his words. What does that even mean? Before I can respond, he's already stepping forward, closing the last gap between us, his tall frame dwarfing me.

"Tell me something, Ms. Watson," he continues, his voice dropping even lower, like a secret between us. "What's your strategy for convincing me you're the right fit? Because, right now, all I see is a woman who's too eager. Too desperate. It's... interesting, but not exactly what I'm looking for."

The air between us thickens, and I can't breathe properly. My heart's doing strange flips in my chest. This man is getting dangerously close to making me forget why I'm here.

My throat dries as I try to steady myself. I force my gaze to stay on his—don't let him see me sweat or see how much his proximity is messing with my head.

I take a slow and deliberate breath to regain control of my thoughts and emotions. "The only thing I'm desperate for is for you to leave my personal space!" I spit back at him, and he immediately steps back with a scowl.

Good.

"I don't need your approval, Mr. Freeman. I came here to

meet with the owner of this resort, Mrs. Ann Freeman, who invited me to interview. I need to impress her, not you." The words come out with more confidence than I feel, but I stand firm.

He looks at me for a moment, his eyes unreadable, before he steps back, nodding slowly as though I've passed some test. But I know better than to think he's finished playing with me.

Men like him always play with their food. And that's precisely how he's looking at me like prey to be devoured.

"Well, that's interesting," he says, the words almost amused. "You're still here. Most people flee once they realize they aren't wanted."

I raise an eyebrow, the corner of my mouth quirking just enough to let him know I'm not backing down despite his put-down. "I don't walk away from challenges, Mr. Freeman," I say, the fire inside me reigniting. "Not when they're this... compelling."

His gaze softens ever so slightly, and I catch the flicker of something more dangerous behind his eyes—a challenge that feels like an invitation. "Compelling, huh?" he murmurs, his lips barely moving. "Careful, Ms. Watson. You might end up getting more than you're asking for."

He's trouble—the kind I don't need. But my honeypot, that wild thing inside me, is not getting the memo. She's doing the absolute most right now, and somehow, I think he knows it.

For a split second, I wonder if I'm getting in over my head. But then, I remind myself. I'm here for the job, not for whatever... this is. I can still hear the leer in Jackson's voice... *work out something personal.* Not happening.

"You should prepare, then," I say, my voice steady despite the heat rising. "Because I always aim for more than what I'm offered."

His lips twitch again like he's fighting a smile, and for the first time, I see the faintest glimmer of respect in his eyes. Then he knocks the wind from my sails.

"No, Ms. Watson. I'm afraid you won't even get the bare minimum this time. None of our family has time to interview you today, but I may call you in a week or two if you're a good girl." His voice is smooth but laced with finality.

Then, with a lethal grace reserved for lions, tigers, and bears, he turns his back on me and walks up the steps of Baycrest, leaving me standing there, both seething and undeniably captivated by his retreating figure."

The hell...

FIVE

You're So Vain

SIERRA

I WATCH IN DISBELIEF AS JABARI FREEMAN WALKS UP the stairs, his purposeful strides taking him farther from me with each step. This man's audacity in dismissing me so effortlessly fuels my determination not to be brushed aside.

Who the hell does he think he is?

I'm not going anywhere. My sister is depending on me, and I can't let this be the end of it.

I move before I can fully process my actions. My heels click against the cobblestone path as I rush after him, my voice slicing through the air like a sharp blade.

"Wait just a minute!" I call out, the edge in my tone betraying my anger. Jabari pauses mid-step, turning slightly to glance back at me with a raised eyebrow. There's that flicker of amusement in his light eyes again, with a glint of curiosity dancing within their depths.

I swiftly close the distance between us, standing directly in his path as I refuse to be ignored. "You can't just walk away from me," I declare, my voice getting higher by the minute.

I feel damn near feral.

"I drove from Anacostia for this interview, and you will not dismiss me because I don't look or speak the way you think I should. You can save that Black elitist bullshit for someone else."

He looks genuinely taken aback and angry as he descends the steps two at a time to get face-to-face with me. All the amusement and curiosity has left his eyes, and now he's all business. "What makes you think this has anything to do with how you look or speak? What makes you think this has anything to do with you at all?"

He smells so good that I almost groan in satisfaction. But I've got to keep it together. I can't forget he's an arrogant asshole who won't even give me the interview I came here for.

"What else could it be? You looked at me and said that no one from your family would interview me." My mind acknowledges that my voice is steadily rising, but I can't stop the train.

"Then you had the nerve to tell me I needed to be a "good girl" and MAYBE I'd get a callback!"

Great, now I'm screaming.

Jabari's jaw tightens, and his hazel eyes darken with frustration and something else I can't quite decipher. His imposing presence grows even more dominant as he leans in slightly. His voice is low and controlled but unmistakable in intensity.

"First of all, lower your voice. We're not outside on the block. This"—he emphasizes with a wild gesturing of his hands above his head—"is a place of business, a luxury resort. I know you may not be familiar with the concept, but it's a place of peace."

I open my mouth to retort, but he cuts me off.

"Furthermore, my decision not to interview you has nothing to do with you, Ms. Watson," he asserts firmly, his voice suddenly laced with sorrow and his tone heavy with emotion. My father passed away two days ago, and our family is grieving the loss. So, no, today is not the day for interviews."

His words hit me hard, robbing me of breath and sapping the defiance and anger I had just seconds ago. My hubris vanishes, replaced by a stark guilt and empathy for the man before me.

"I-I had no idea," I stammer, my voice faltering as I struggle to recover from the sudden shift. I feel like a complete jerk for my earlier outburst. Tentatively, almost instinctually, I reach out and place my hand over his, hoping my genuine regret will come through. "I'm so sorry for your loss."

Silence hangs between us, thick with the weight of his words and the realization of my misjudgment. Jabari looks down at where my hand rests on his, and for a moment, his expression softens, revealing a flicker of understanding beneath the stoic mask he's worn. I feel another pang of guilt course through me. My temper often gets the best of me, and now I regret my haste and the resulting insensitivity.

When he jerks his hand away from mine, the sudden movement feels like a slap. His reaction is harsh, as if my touch burned him. A painful lump forms in my throat, and the sting of rejection hits me.

Before I can grasp what's happening, his voice strikes me like a punch to the gut. "I'm glad you finally understand—that not everything revolves around you," he spits, each word sharp and laced with bitterness. The sneer on his face makes my stomach churn. "But don't you dare think your petty problems compare to the grief my family is enduring? You want a job? Well, I want my father back."

The weight of his words crushes me, and I flinch as he

continues, his tone cutting deep. "Now, please leave and show some damn respect."

His words feel like ice water, momentarily freezing me as I'm blindsided by the chill in his voice. He's correct; I should leave, but the bite in his tone—cutting through the tense silence —strikes deep.

I know all too well the pain of losing a parent.

With a nod, I step back, giving him the space he's asking for. The air is thick with unspoken tension, and as I turn to walk away, I don't even know this man, but his grief hits me harder than I expected. He's hurting, and for some reason, that stirs something in me—something I can't quite shake.

As I reach the cobblestone path leading back to the driveway, I look over my shoulder, wondering if he's watching me leave. It's ridiculous, I know. But even now, I can't help but wonder if he notices how I walk and appreciates the curve of my hips. I should be thinking about how to help Shana, but I can only focus on him. It's wild. I was only with him for fifteen minutes, and I'm pretty sure he could turn my whole world upside down in less than an hour if he got the chance.

That's why this may be for the best. There's no way I'm sticking around here. I'll find another way to help Shana.

As I reach my car, ready to leave the scene, I see an older but striking woman coming from behind the house, flanked by two tall, serious-looking men. My steps slow as I watch them. The woman is Ann Freeman, whom I recognize from the photos online. The two identical men beside her look so much like Jabari that I stop dead.

They walk right past him, who's standing at the top of the driveway, clearly seething, and head straight toward me. The resemblance is so strong that I have to blink a few times. Then it hits me: Ann Freeman must have more sons. Sons who are just as breathtaking and commanding as Jabari.

Does Ann Freeman breed Big Daddy Energy? Because, my Gawd, they are fine.

I shake off my surprise, taking a deep breath to clear my head, my fingers curling around the car door handle as embarrassment and regret cloud my thoughts. All I want is to get out of here, to escape. But just as I'm about to pull the door open, Ann's warm voice calls out to me, cutting through the air like sunshine breaking through dark clouds.

"Miss Watson, hold on a moment," she says, her voice soft yet commanding, as she glides down the steps toward me. Something about her—graceful, dignified, and kind—immediately eases the tension in my chest, even as my heart still feels heavy with all the unspoken emotions swirling around.

"You must be Miss Watson," she says gently. "I'm Ann Freeman, and I'm so sorry I'm late for our appointment." She steps closer, the space between us shrinking with every movement, before she waves her two bodyguards—or sons—back a few paces. As she nears, I catch the faintest scent of her perfume—jasmine and vanilla, sweet and soothing. "I know you came down from Washington. I truly appreciate you making the effort."

She turns slightly to her two imposing sons behind her, who stand tall and regal, just like Jabari. "These are my sons, Asa and Amir." Her voice softens with an apology. "It looks like you've already spoken with Jabari. He's been away for the past ten years, and I'm just glad to lay eyes on him. So, I'm unsure how much help he could be. I would have never sent him over to talk to you." She gives a side-eye to the top of the steps where Jabari is still standing.

That mean mammoth has been away from his mama and family for ten years? *Figures.*

I pull my hand away from the car handle and turn fully to face her, and she continues. She's stunning, and there's something so genuine about her—if sincerity had a face, it would be the smile on this woman's lips.

"Anyway, I'm sorry I'm late. Please forgive me; I'm never tardy."

Despite everything she's going through—losing her husband today—she's trying to ease my discomfort. Who does that? No one. I certainly didn't care about Jabari or the reasons his family might have for canceling my interview until he told me his father had passed away. I want to be graceful like her. Now, I feel awful for not being anything like her at all.

"No, no, don't apologize," I mumble, my voice barely a whisper. "I understand. You... your family... your loss... two days—"

But that's as far as I get before the words crack, and I burst into tears. Somehow, my grief over the anniversary of my mother's death has melded into theirs, and I'm an emotional mess.

Before I know it, I'm in her arms, overwhelmed by the weight of the day. Her sons, Asa and Amir, step forward, their eyes filled with quiet concern. Despite their imposing size, they're oddly comforting, like anchors in a storm. Ann's voice is soft and steady as she murmurs soothing words, guiding me to a nearby bench under a tree. Her touch feels like a lifeline, steadying me as a wave of emotion crashes over me.

"Oh, sweetheart," she says, her voice warm and calming. "There's no need to cry. You haven't done anything wrong. You didn't know my husband, and you certainly didn't know he was going to pick today to die. Hell, I didn't know that, and he's been by my side for over forty-two years."

She finishes with a soft laugh, and despite the tears streaming down my face, I can't help but smile. If she's not falling apart, then why am I?

I try to pull myself together, wiping away tears that don't want to stop.

Why am I crying like this? I've always prided myself on being strong and composed. But today, the anniversary of my mother's death, the encounter with Jabari—his grief wrapped in a shell of grumpiness—and now Ann's unexpected kindness... something inside me has cracked, and I can't figure out what it is.

Sitting on the bench, surrounded by a family that radiates warmth and understanding, a small bubble of laughter escapes my lips through the tears. The sheer absurdity of it all tickles me, if only for a second. It's so unlike me, and yet... here I am.

Ann places a hand on my shoulder, her gaze steady as she looks me in the eye. It's as if she's figured out the answer to all my problems. She gently cups my face in her hands and gives me the best advice I've ever heard in that soft, confident way that I bet only she has.

Her son Jabari sure doesn't have it.

"Miss Watson," she says, her voice gentle but firm. "Laughing when you want to cry is a sign of resilience. It's your way of saying I'm still here. I'm still fighting. Never stop laughing, and never stop fighting."

I swallow hard, nodding slowly. Her words settle deep in my chest, and then my thoughts drift to Shana, to why I'm here. I think about everything I need this job for and how desperately I need it. Then, as if in a trance, I laugh. Not a polite chuckle, but a deep, almost desperate laugh, like my life depends on it.

Maybe it does.

SIX

Nothin' You Can Do About It

JABARI

Delight isn't a word I usually use, but it's the only way to describe the laughter flowing between Mother and Sierra as I step back down the steps and draw closer.

One minute, Sierra was crying in her arms, and now my mother is wiping her tears and laughing alongside her.

I stop a few yards away with my gaze locked on her, and the world seems to fade.

The first thing I noticed when I spoke to her was that the auburn curls on her head caught the breeze, bouncing around her face like a fiery halo while she spoke. The freckles scattered across her sun-kissed skin remind me of constellations twinkling in the night sky, and I swear I want to count and kiss every single one. To top it all off, she's wearing a bright yellow sundress that wraps around her full bosom in a way that makes me want to nap there.

And her ass... my dick hardens just thinking about how much time I'd like to spend back there licking, teasing, and smacking.

For a moment, touching her became the only thing that mattered, and that was a problem. The last time I felt this way, I did something stupid, like asking Vee to marry me, which was my biggest mistake.

I was cold to Sierra and evasive about my reasons for refusing to interview her. I wanted her to leave, but the Siren only sang louder.

I've got to shake this instant and overwhelming attraction to her off because her vulnerability calls to me.

When my mother came, I hated seeing Sierra cry; the sobs did weird things to my chest area that I didn't like one bit—but watching my brothers pat her on the back and touch her! That's too much.

I should be the one consoling her, not them!

The scene before me was like a live wire to my senses—a stark contrast to the storm cloud I am ready to unleash.

I march over and stand amid their party of laughs. "Miss Watson," I say, interrupting without a hint of apology. "I thought you were leaving. As you can imagine, our family has things to prepare in private."

My tone is deliberate, leaving no room for debate. I watch Sierra's smile falter, her eyes, the color of autumn leaves, narrowing slightly at the abrupt change in weather. They're—amber and warm—holding a depth that pulls at something deep inside me. There's intelligence in them, kindness too, and it's impossible not to be drawn in, like a moth to a flame. And her lips... those full, inviting lips curve down into a pout that makes me want to wrap my fist around all that wild hair and take her mouth for all it's worth. I can only imagine how they must taste—soft and sweet, like ripe peaches under the summer sun. And it pisses me off!

She's innocent and warm now that my mother has arrived on the scene, but I'm not fooled by her freckled charm or how those sexy, wild curls frame her perfect face. I've seen how quickly a storm can roll over the Chesapeake Bay, so I know better than to get caught in one.

And mark my words—Sierra Watson is a Category 5 hurricane.

"Jabari, surely—" Mother starts, but I cut her off with a look. It's harsh, maybe too harsh for my mother, but necessary. Sierra must go—for the sake of my sanity.

"Due to our recent loss," the words curt and cold, like the bay in January. "Mother, even you would have to admit that we have more pertinent family business to tend to than a trivial interview."

I'm clenching my teeth so hard I can feel the muscles in my jaw twitching, a silent sign of the tight hold I have on everything —my emotions, my thoughts, my dick. Sierra's gaze flicks to my face, studying me like a puzzle to solve. I can almost see the wheels turning in her head, weighing whether to push back or pull away. I'm betting on the former. Resilience practically pulses from her, and I'm sure she won't back down easily.

"Understood," she says finally, her voice steady. But a glint in her eyes tells me she's not conceding the game, just this round. And something about that both irks and excites me.

"Family first, right?" The corner of her mouth tilts up in what could be the start of a smile—or a smirk. I'm beginning to see that it's hard to tell with Sierra Watson.

I can feel my twin brothers' amusement at her sarcasm practically vibrating off the trees. Asa snickers under his breath; Amir's grin is wide, knowing they can see something I can't. My baby brothers are a pain in my ass on a good day, but now that they get to watch a beautiful woman attempt to take me down a peg or two, they're in hog heaven.

I glare at them, daring them to keep laughing. So, of course, they do. *Assholes.*

Then I turn back to the Siren sent to torment me. "Always," I confirm, not backing down an inch. "Which is why you need to leave. This is a time for family, not a random potential employee."

My mother gasps and straightens like an ageless queen in her realm, her eyes narrowing into slits sharp enough to cut through steel. My last comment was rude, and my mother hates rudeness. I do, too, but Sierra seems to take me out of character. That's why she needs to go before I do something crazy, like kiss that smart mouth of hers into submission.

But I also recognize a quiet storm brewing beneath my mother's calm surface. I know better than to challenge anything she says next.

"Miss Watson," she begins, her voice soft yet filled with authority. "My apologies for my son's... abruptness. It's his first day at the resort in ten years, and he's not up to speed on how we do things. She stands and adjusts her silk shawl. "But you see, my dear," she continues, her gaze shifting between Sierra and me, "Jabari's bark is worse than his bite. Underneath that stern exterior lies a heart weighed down by grief."

My mother's words linger in the air, unexpected and raw, cutting through the tension with a softness I wasn't prepared for. I can feel a spark of irritation rise, but I quickly bury it, hiding behind a mask of indifference. Grief? It's a luxury I can't afford right now, not with the constant, crushing weight of my father's absence and what it means for my future pressing down on me.

Sierra's eyes soften, and for a moment, there's a glimmer of something like understanding in them—an unexpected empathy that makes my chest tighten. It unsettles me; she seems to see the storm inside me for what it is. I'm not used to letting anyone in, especially not someone I barely know, someone who seems to peel back my defenses with every look.

My mother, always the keen observer, catches Sierra's change in expression and, with a hint of wry humor, turns to me and adds, "You never did listen to my advice about laughter being the best medicine, did you?" She teases, her voice light, "Always choosing brooding over banter." A small smile tugs at her lips, a fleeting moment of levity amid everything heavy hanging between us. Then she comes over and takes my hand.

"Jabari," she continues, her gaze steady and filled with unshakable grace. "If you're going to lead this family now, you need to know that your father didn't build this resort just for business—it's a testament to our sense of community and culture. We keep these doors open, no matter the storm, because that's what he would've done. We need an activities director, and I think we've found one." She adds a wink, her words a quiet reassurance wrapped in grief and strength.

"Ma..." I growl, but she raises a hand, silencing me with the gesture. Then she turns to the woman who's turned my life upside down in under an hour.

"Miss Watson," my mother says, her voice steady and sure, "Chesapeake Heights is more than a retreat; it's a sanctuary for those cast aside, a legacy of battles fought and won." Her eyes drift toward the bay waters beyond our home. "Even now, as we mourn my husband, we honor his legacy by pressing on. That's the heart of what we do here. We press on."

The air between us is thick with unspoken things—my brothers' amusement, my mother's unwavering resolve, and Sierra's discomfort, a stranger caught in the crossfire of a duty that spans generations.

And then there's me, standing in awe of the quiet power of

a matriarch calming storms with a single word. Ann Freeman might be half my size, but she carries more weight than I'll ever bring to bear.

"Now, Miss Watson," my mother continues, her eyes locking with mine. Would you like to see the rest of the resort for yourself?" Her invitation is a challenge, a test I can feel deep in my bones.

Sierra looks at me and my mother before squaring her shoulders and pasting on a sexy smile.

"Yes, Ms. Freeman, I'd love to."

SEVEN

Sweet Green Fields

SIERRA

FROM THE STORMY GLARE JABARI GIVES ME, IT'S evident he's holding back some choice words.

He's got to be one of the grumpiest men I've ever met. I know he's grieving, but I get the feeling that jackass is his natural state of being.

His mama shut him, and his rude behavior down, and part of me wants to laugh, but I won't. Not with the way he's staring at me—if looks could kill, my butt would be a pile of ash right now.

I should've told Mrs. Freeman no when she asked me to tour the grounds. From my job and training, I know Jabari's working through his grief in the only way he knows how, and I'm just the unlucky target for all that frustration.

But as much as I want to turn around and run home, the

flicker of hesitation in me quickly gives way to something stronger. It's curiosity and maybe a bit of attraction.

Besides, I need this job.

And then there's Ann, as she told me to call her. She's a part of Chesapeake Heights, woven into its very fabric, like the land itself. How could I possibly say no to her? She may be working through her grief by talking about her husband's work.

"All right," I exhale, my decision solidifying under her expectant gaze. "I'm ready whenever you are."

"Wonderful," she sighs with a warmth that soothes the tension in the air. She links her arm with mine, and we step into the cool embrace of the salty bay breeze, leaving Jabari behind to stew in his disapproval.

As Ann leads the way, the resort stretches before me—alive with history, a testament to resilience and grace. It's like stepping into another time, where the echoes of those who came before still breathe.

"Chesapeake Heights has always been a beacon," Ann begins, her voice thick with pride. "When our people had nowhere else safe to go, they came here."

I look around, and the ancient oaks' branches stretch out like arms from ancestors long past, offering a silent welcome. The waves kiss the shore, carrying the dreams of generations who sought solace and hope on these warm, sandy beaches.

"Your husband's family built something incredible," I murmur, my voice awed. I am caught up in the weight of the story unfolding around me. Truth be told, I wanted to be a history major. Instead, I chose psychology and minored in African-American Studies. I didn't know how I'd get a job with a history degree, and I admired the psychologist who helped me with my grief as a teenager. This job will scratch my historical itch, for sure.

She nods. "Yes, they did. Marcus and his ancestors believed

freedom was more than a word," Ann says, her voice softening, the weight of memory settling over her like a protective cloak. "It was a place where one could simply be." Her eyes shimmer with unshed tears, but her smile remains radiant, as bright as the sun above us.

That smile, infectious as it is, tugs at my heart. Despite the current heaviness of life, I find myself smiling, too. It's only for a fleeting moment but a spark of something. Maybe there's a place for me in this legacy of battles fought and victories won.

As we walk, I feel Jabari's presence before I see him, his shadow a faint whisper behind Ann's confident steps. When I steal a glance over my shoulder, there he is—hands clasped tightly behind his broad back, his expression unreadable but his posture screaming control. He's a silent guardian, watchful and unrelenting.

I whip my head back around, pretending not to notice him, but the heat of his gaze burns into the small of my back like a brand. It's steady and searing; I feel it no matter how much I try to shake it off. I bite my lip, fighting the overwhelming urge to glance again, refusing to give him the satisfaction of knowing how much his stare rattles me.

Instead, I trudge along the uneven trail, willing myself to stay composed, but fate has other plans. My foot catches on a big, stubborn, and perfectly placed root to send me sprawling.

Time slows as I lurch forward, bracing for the harsh sting of dirt and gravel against my skin. But it never comes.

Instead, strong arms yank me back, wrapping around me like a vice and holding me steady before the ground can claim me. His touch impacts me like a lightning strike, sending electricity coursing through me as I gasp at the warmth of his body pressed against mine. His chest is solid, his grip firm, and for a moment, I lean into him, caught between the safety of his embrace and the unmistakable charge sparking in the air between us.

"Careful, Siren," Jabari murmurs, his voice low and rough against my ear. The way he says it sends shivers down my spine; his tone is full of something I can't quite name but feel everywhere. "We can't have you hurting yourself."

Before I can absorb the warmth of his breath against my skin and the solidity of his presence behind me, he straightens me up and steps back. His hands drop away as quickly as they arrived, leaving me cold and off balance in more ways than one.

I catch my breath, my heart racing for reasons that have nothing to do with the near fall and everything to do with the man standing behind me.

"My name is Sierra," I mutter as I move past him.

Ann continues, blissfully unaware of the hot mess unfolding behind her. When she suddenly stops, she turns and smirks at her son but doesn't say a word. Instead, she gestures to a green clearing encircled by towering, venerable oaks. "And here is where we host our annual jazz festival," she says. "Every first week of July, music becomes the heartbeat of Chesapeake Heights."

"Sounds amazing," I reply, my voice faltering just a little, caught in the pull of Jabari's eyes. He might as well be wrapped in caution tape, the way he stands so still, so controlled. His fitted tee clings to his muscular frame like a second skin, and every inch of him exudes power and restraint.

I want him to unravel.

"Sierra, are you all right?" Ann's concerned voice breaks through my reverie.

"Absolutely," I lie, offering a brittle smile. The truth is, Jabari makes me nervous, not because of his brooding demeanor, but because there's something in his guarded gaze that threatens to scale the walls I've built around my heart with ease.

I'll never give a man my heart again. After that stunt Thomas pulled, I'm good. I don't need false promises or fake concern. I've got my hands full with Shana. I think Thomas also hated how much I had to bail her out. But he was an only child; he didn't understand our bond.

Now, I only invite a man into my bed for fun and promptly ask them to leave.

I have built a fortress around my heart, hoping and praying that it is strong enough to keep out the chaos that comes with men like Jabari Freeman.

I know he's trying to intimidate me with his proximity. But as a public school psychologist, I've faced down teenagers armed with nothing but raging hormones and smart mouths. A stoic giant won't shake me.

"Let's move on to the restaurants," Ann suggests, her warmth chasing away the chill of Jabari's scrutiny.

"Lead the way," I say, squaring my shoulders as I step forward, determined.

"Are you a fan of history, Sierra?" Ann asks, her kind eyes studying mine.

"Yes! It was my minor in college." My admission makes Jabari's eyes land on me in surprise. I roll my eyes at his reaction, "History is what shapes us," I answer, the words both a shield and a lance. "If we don't face it, we will never learn the lessons we need for the future. We will always know which way to go in life if we're willing to listen to the wisdom from the past."

"Indeed," she nods, a knowing smile tugging at the corners of her lips.

We round another corner, and I catch Jabari shifting uncomfortably, his expression unreadable. My words rattled him. I don't know what he's running from in his past, but he doesn't want to face it. I have a feeling that his father's death is bringing it all to the surface.

The tour continues, with history seeping from every stone and blade of grass, wrapping around me like a cloak. Though Jabari's presence looms like a gathering storm, I walk on, refusing to let the shadows dictate the path of my sun.

"Back in sixty -six," Ann begins, gesturing to a grand oak, "that's where the NAACP held protest planning meetings and sang freedom songs. This resort was more than a getaway; it was a civil rights command center."[Paula Gru3]

"Sounds like you all were writing history, not just living it," I quip, trying to keep the mood light, even though Shana's shadow still hangs over me. I can't get sucked into loving this tour so much that I forget to secure this job.

"Indeed, we were," Ann replies, her tone colored with a chuckle. "And we're still writing chapters."

I admire her. She's a matriarch scripting her family's legacy against changing times. I can only imagine the corporate offers they get for a private beachfront property like this. She's strong. She has the type of strength I need, for Shana's sake.

"Sierra, have you ever felt the weight of familial duty?" Ann's question catches me off guard, her eyes holding mine as if she can read the subtext of my life.

"Every day," I admit, thinking of the promises I made to my mother and the burden of protecting my sister from her demons. "It's heavy," I reluctantly admit, catching Jabari staring at me.

"Ah, but that weight can also be a foundation," Ms. Ann says, "from it, we build futures," she says, lightly touching the bark of the oak, a gentle reminder of perseverance.

"Building futures," I echo, longing for something lasting,

free from the debts and dangers that chase us. Maybe, just maybe, here, amid this sanctuary of history and hope, I can find the tools to build something of my own.

"Come," Ann beckons, leading me toward a sun-dappled clearing. "There's more to see, and each corner of this land tells a different story."

Her stories weave through the air, a tapestry of struggle and triumph that wraps around me, offering warmth where Jabari's watchful gaze has only offered chill. Yet, his silent vigilance also feels secure—like he'd wrestle a bear if it came after his mother... or me.

"Your family's stories are inspiring," I say, meaning every word. "They remind me that no matter what comes at us, we've got to stand tall—like these oaks."

"Exactly," Ann agrees, her smile a ray of sunlight breaking through the canopy of leaves. "And we must remember to extend branches of support to those who need them."

Branches of support. I wonder if this is an offer, a sign of something more. I dare to hope I've found an ally in Ann who understands the weight of familial responsibility and the fierce love that drives me.

"Thank you," I whisper, feeling gratitude stir within me. "For sharing this place with me."

"Thank you for listening," she responds. "The stories only live on when ears are willing to hear them."

As Ann speaks of the past, I can't help but think of my story, tangled up with Shana's reckless choices. But here, beneath the protective boughs of Chesapeake Heights, I allow myself to believe in a different ending—one where legacies aren't chains but wings.

"Your questions, Sierra—they're not just surface-level," Ann says, suddenly interrupting my thoughts and catching me off guard. "You have an eye for what truly matters."

"Or maybe I'm just nosy," I joke, and Jabari grunts. But his mother's words stir something inside me—something warm, a flutter of validation I can't ignore.

"Nosiness is a virtue around here," she says with a wink. "It means you care enough to look beyond the obvious. I believe you're a budding historian."

I laugh, ignoring Jabari's wordless dig.

"Sierra, this place needs someone with your tendency to honor the past," she says, pausing to run a hand along the rough bark of an ancient tree, her voice steady. "Someone who can mix something modern like pickleball tournaments with the sensibility of historic nature walks."

"Are you offering me the job?" I ask, half amused, half anxious.

"Consider it an invitation," Ann replies, her eyes sparkling with warmth and challenge. "A chance to be part of something greater than yourself. To help shape a future rooted in the legacy of this land."

"I would be honored," I say, my voice steady, grounding myself in the promise of this new chapter. "To help preserve and nurture this place, to see it thrive."

Ann's smile widens, and a quiet agreement passes between us as if she knows something I'm just beginning to understand. "Then it's settled. You'll start in one week. We celebrate and bury my Marcus in six days on Sunday morning- a tradition for the Freeman family. You, my dear, will start first thing on Monday. Jabari will ensure you're settled in on your first day and understand your duties."

When his name is mentioned, my gaze shifts toward Jabari, standing nearby. His expression is cold, but something about his stillness makes my heart skip a beat.

He meets my eyes for only a second before turning and walking away. It's brief, almost dismissive, but I don't care. Not anymore. I'm determined to be the best activities director Chesapeake Heights Bay Resort has ever had, and I won't let his feelings about me being here throw me off course. This is one win, one opportunity, that I refuse to forfeit.

EIGHT

If You Could Read My Mind

JABARI

ONE WEEK LATER

THE SHARP RING OF MY PHONE YANKS ME FROM MY sleep, and I answer without opening my eyes.

"Hello," I growl, my voice thick with exhaustion and a hangover that has my head pounding.

Lola, our security guard, huffs in response. "I thought you'd want to know; Miss Sierra Watson is on her way to Baycrest. She says she's set to meet with you at eight a.m."

"Fuck," I mutter under my breath. "What time is it?"

Lola chuckles softly. "Seven fifty-eight a.m. Rise and shine, Mr. Freeman." The line goes dead as she hangs up.

I force my eyes open, and the morning light slices through the blinds, a brutal reminder that rest doesn't find me often. With a groan, I drag myself out of bed, the weight of yesterday's suit still clinging to me like a second skin—heavy, uncomfortable, a stark reminder of everything lost.

My father's funeral had been a portrait of elegance and restraint, a somber affair that could have been lifted from the pages of Chesapeake Heights' storied past. We were dressed in black, just as he had requested. True to form, Marcus Freeman had orchestrated every detail of the memorial service, from the speeches to the songs the choir would sing.

For the service itself, my mother, my four siblings, and I held it together. We loved Papa, so we did what he would've wanted—kept the stiff upper lip. No dramatics. No emotional outbursts. And certainly, no fighting.

But the repast? That was a different story altogether. The family's façade cracked once crab cakes and Corona entered the equation. What should've been a time for healing turned into a battle over what should have united us: the damn resort.

"We're going to keep it," my mother had said, her voice laced with the weight of generations. "It's your father's legacy. I won't let you throw it away simply because you've never committed to anything but the military."

"Legacy doesn't pay the bills," I snapped, my voice as sharp as the creases in my black suit.

There was no room for sentimentality in that conversation, no strategy that could cut through the fortress of nostalgia that seemed to blind them all. I'd spent the entire week before my father's funeral going over the books—ledgers I'm sure he kept from my mother and siblings. The resort was bleeding money, and he insisted on slapping Band-Aids made of pride and history over a problem that needed a real solution. We could not afford to do the same. So I kept going, even though my mother looked like she wanted to slice me open and roast me on the spot.

"Ma, I'm committed to ensuring our family survives the

next two or three storms we know are coming. We must reinforce all the resort structures—about thirty buildings—with steel and hurricane-proof glass. We need to strengthen the storm barriers at the beach. And all that costs capital we don't have. We're bleeding out our future for sentimentality, and I won't let my father's work get sold off to the bank in foreclosure."

Then my brother Malik chimed in, his voice a mix of anger and resentment. "What the hell do you know about anything, Jabari? You left ten years ago and never looked back. If Ma doesn't want to sell, we're not selling. And if you don't want to stick around to help us figure out how to make it happen, you can get in that Black Beast of yours and drive straight back to VA Beach."

I just stared at him, taking in the wild mane of twisted hair and that piercing gaze he had perfected over the years—one that could unsettle even the most steadfast souls. There he stood, nothing more than a self-righteous prick wrapped in an expensive West African day suit, speaking as if his words were gospel truth. But I knew better.

Malik never finished anything he started—not even his degree from Morehouse. His words were like honey, sweet but shallow, dripping from his lips easily. Charismatic, sure, with a charm that could light up a room, but beneath it all, there was a man who couldn't see a task through to the end if it smacked him in the face.

And then there was his mysterious military discharge. The sealed records, the hushed whispers that followed him like ghosts of a past we weren't supposed to investigate. Whatever happened during his time in service remained a mystery, and every time I looked at him, that gnawing curiosity ate away at me.

And now, this fool wanted to tell me what to do! He came

down from his Harlem hideout once a year to spy on our events coordinator, Jade Jackson. Amara thought he came down to kiss Mama and Papa's ass, but I knew better. My brother has never cared about pleasing my parents. And he sure as hell doesn't want to be responsible for this resort. Nope, it only took me following him one day last week to find out what he was really up to—some pussy.

I swear if his words about me leaving hadn't been so damn accurate, I might've whooped him right there in the clubhouse dining room. But instead, I did what I do best—I fled.

I found a bar in Lusby, the next town over, and I drank away my frustration. But I'm too old for hangovers, and now, as I drag myself out of bed, I'm paying the price.

I stumble to the mirror, glaring at my reflection. With my dark skin and tailored beard— I look every inch the stoic leader, the Navy SEAL who's faced hell and come out the other side without flinching. But right now, standing here, I feel like I'm about to walk into a war zone unarmed.

Sierra Watson. Howard University alum, school psychologist, and a damn force of nature at this point, I've memorized her resume.

She starts today as the activities director, and my mother put her on my caseload to train. I haven't seen her in six days, but I've thought about her every night with my hand wrapped around my stiff, aching dick. I haven't jerked off this much since I was a teenager.

It's got to be some cosmic joke. Her walking into my life now is when I need distraction the least. She doesn't just push my buttons; she rewires the entire panel.

And truthfully, she scares the hell out of me. Her freckles and wildfire curls call to my senses, demanding my attention when I know I shouldn't give it. The last time she was in my presence, all I could think about was throwing her down on the nearest surface and tasting every inch of her glorious body, unraveling her in every way possible until she came apart in my hands.

"Stay strong," I mutter, but it sounds unconvincing.

The day she showed up on our doorstep, I fully intended to shut her out, to dismiss her with a cold glance and carry on. And I did. But she still managed to slide past every defense I've built over the years like they were made of smoke. Now? I can't afford to let that happen again. Not today. Not ever.

"Hell no," I growl, as much to myself as to the man staring back at me. Even as I pull on my black fitted jeans and T-shirt, I know Sierra Watson is the trouble you can't lock out. She's the storm on the horizon, one that promises chaos—and maybe, just maybe, something worth getting soaked for.

"Keep Control, Jabari," I coach myself as I hurry downstairs. But deep down, I know the truth. My heart, that traitor within my chest, is already set to betray me when I see the first flash of her defiant smile.

I make it downstairs before she arrives, but now I wish I'd waited in my office and had the receptionist send her back so I could give myself another round of pep talks to fortify my will.

But before I can retreat, Sierra Watson marches into the Chesapeake Heights Resort's staff office like a summer storm— hot, unpredictable, and impossible to ignore. And damn, if she doesn't look like trouble wrapped in a package too tempting to resist.

Her light-blue polo shirt, emblazoned with the resort's logo, hugs her curves in a way that should violate workplace dress codes. Those khaki shorts, snug and too short, leaving just enough to the imagination while making it clear that whatever higher power designed her wasn't playing fair.

My throat tightens as my eyes betray me, cataloging every inch of her—from those long, toned legs to the faint sheen of sweat on her collarbone. *Focus, Jabari.* But my body has its agenda, and I can feel the heat rising in more ways than one.

"Good morning, Mr. Freeman," she says, her voice sweet and airy, like she doesn't know she's a walking distraction. The faint smirk tugging at the corner of her mouth tells me she knows precisely the chaos she's causing. "Sure is hot today, isn't it?"

And then, as if to punctuate the point, she fans herself, drawing attention to the open collar of her polo, where two buttons are undone. The slight sheen on her skin glistens in the light, and my mind conjures thoughts I have no business entertaining—thoughts like licking that moisture from her body, inch by inch.

Damn, now I'm sporting a semi in my pants.

My balls will be as blue as that damn polo she's wearing.

This cannot happen. Not here. Not now.

"Let's get one thing straight, Ms. Watson," I snap, sharper than I intend. The bite in my voice is more for me than her, a desperate attempt to rein myself in. "Here at Chesapeake Heights, we value professionalism and structure. Your shorts? Way too short." I gesture vaguely toward her legs, my frustration flaring when her eyebrows arch, daring me to elaborate. "And your shirt should be buttoned up to the collar. Otherwise, our distinguished guests won't take you seriously."

The words taste bitter, even as they leave my mouth. I don't believe half of them. She looks damn good, and that's the real problem. *My problem.* One I didn't ask for.

Her expression doesn't falter. Instead, she buttons her polo with deliberate slowness, her curls bouncing as she nods. "Of course," she replies smoothly, not a hint of irritation in her tone. "I'll find longer shorts. And please, call me Sierra. Now, what should I start with? I'm eager to learn."

Oh, I'll call you Sierra, all right. But there's no way I'm letting her off that easily.

I narrow my eyes, crossing my arms over my chest. "Why do you need this job so badly?" The question tumbles out before I can stop myself. It's been gnawing at me since she applied. "You're a school psychologist in DCPS—top of your class. Good salary. Why spend your summer entertaining tourists who think they're above you? Seems like a waste of your time."

Her lips twitch, but she doesn't back down. "Why does it matter?" she counters, her voice light and too quick to be genuine. Maybe I want to save for a house."

I lean closer, invading her space, watching her reaction like a hawk. "You already own a house," I state coldly.

For the first time, I see a flicker of surprise in her eyes—just a flicker, but enough to let me know I've hit a nerve. She quickly recovers, tilting her head with a smirk that makes my blood boil.

"Been checking up on me, have you?" she asks, feigned amusement lacing her words. "What are you, obsessed with me or something?"

I take a steadying breath, my jaw tightening as I wrestle with the truth. *Yes, Sierra, I'm obsessed with you. And it's making me insane.*

But I won't give her that satisfaction.

"I'm not obsessed with you," I say coolly, each word deliberate, like I'm trying to convince myself more than her. "I do my homework. This resort is my family's legacy, and I'm not about to let just anyone work here—especially not someone with as many question marks as you."

Her smirk deepens, and I swear I see amusement flicker in her eyes. She enjoys this—enjoys seeing me off-balance.

"So tell me, Sierra," I press, my voice lowering into a

dangerous growl. "What's the real reason you're here? Because I don't buy the 'saving for a house' story for a second."

For a moment, just a moment, the mask slips. I catch a flash of vulnerability, a crack in her armor, before she slams it shut.

"Like I said, I'm saving for a house. That's all you need to know," she says, stepping back and tilting her chin up, her defiance unmistakable. "Now, will you give me my assignments, or do you just want to keep invading my privacy?"

Her audacity pushes me to the edge, but I don't flinch. She's good. Too good. And it pisses me off even more.

She's *playing* me. Playing me like I'm sure she plays every other man she needs something from, and I'm *damn* tired of it.

This isn't over. I'll get my answers one way or another. But for now, I let it slide. "Fine," I bite out, turning to the task. "Follow me. Pay attention." I say, my voice steady, though my mind's racing with a hundred questions. I lead her through the tasks ahead, my focus razor-sharp. No room for distractions today. Not when she's standing there, looking like that.

"As the activities director, you're not just coordinating events. You're managing the soul of this place—keeping guests engaged, entertained, and coming back for more. You'll need to keep an eye on the daily itinerary. I'm leaving in a few weeks to go back home to VA. You must pay attention and learn everything you can while I'm here."

Telling her I'm leaving leaves a bitter taste in my mouth. I know I must, but for some reason, it doesn't seem as appealing and urgent as it once did. Ignoring the churning in my gut, I continue.

"We've got morning yoga on the beach at eight a.m. sharp, followed by a sandcastle competition for the kids. After lunch, there's the scenic boat tour. You'll be handling guest requests for excursions, ensuring everything goes smoothly."

Her eyes flick up to meet mine, and I see the curiosity mixed with that damnable spark of confidence. Damn her for looking so capable, so eager—so beautiful. I push the thought aside and focus on the job.

"Then you've got the cocktail-making class at three. You'll need to ensure the bartenders have their materials prepped and that guests enjoy a good time. After that, there's the sunset paddleboarding session. I expect you to oversee everything—help set up, check in with the guests, and deal with any issues. And don't forget the evening bonfire on the beach, complete with live music and s'mores. You're the point person for everything, Sierra."

Her lips twitch like she's holding back a smile, and I can't tell if my detailed list of duties amuses her or if she's imagining how soon she can escape this mountain of tasks. But I'm not giving her an inch. Not when she looks like she might unravel me with one glance.

"The resort's success depends on these events and you," I add, my voice lowering as the words hang between us. "So you'll need to stay sharp, handle the pressure, and"—I pause just for a beat, letting the tension coil tighter between us—"make sure that every guest leaves here with more than they expected. Every moment, Sierra, every experience matters."

I see the flicker in her eyes—a flash of determination that reminds me why my mother put her on my radar in the first place. She's capable, intelligent, and everything I don't want her to be. She takes the task seriously, nodding intently.

"Got it," she replies, her voice light but resolute. "What's next?"

Damn her for making it look so easy.

"Next, you'll organize the staff training for the week, ensuring everyone knows their role. You'll shadow our event coordinator, Jade until you get the hang of things. After that, it's your show, Sierra. Don't let my family down."

Something in the way she stands there, looking up at me with those wild curls bouncing with every movement, makes me question whether I have control over this situation. My clipped sentences become terse barks when she questions a policy or suggests an alternative approach. She doesn't cower, though, not Sierra. She meets my gaze head-on, challenging me without saying a word.

That shit turns me the hell on.

But I won't let it show. Not now. Not when I have her under my command, even if it feels like she's pulling the strings.

"Let's see what you can do with all that," I say, my voice a low growl, barely betraying the crackling tension between us.

She smiles then, the kind of smile that promises nothing but trouble—and everything I want. "I'll give it my best shot, Mr. Freeman."

And just like that, I know that every moment with her from here on out will be a battle of wills.

But damn, I'm already addicted to the fight.

NINE

Before I Let Go

SIERRA

THE DOOR TO JABARI'S OFFICE SLAMS BEHIND ME with a satisfying *thud*, echoing like a punctuation mark on my simmering rage. *Insufferable* feels too polite a word for that man. *Arrogant* fits better, but even that doesn't quite capture his sheer audacity. My muttered string of unrepeatable names trails off as my steps quicken, each fueled by indignation.

So caught up in my internal tirade, I don't see her until I nearly barrel right into her.

"Whoa there!"

The voice stops me short, and I look up to find a stunning woman standing in my path. Petite in stature but commanding in presence, she's got a jet-black pixie cut so sharp and chic it could grace the cover of a fashion magazine. Her deep brown skin glows, and her high cheekbones, cupid's bow lips, and sharp jawline give her a look that's as effortless as it is striking. She's dressed in a fitted blue-and-white seersucker blazer over a Chesapeake Heights T-shirt and tailored slacks. She looks like she belongs here as if she owns the room without trying.

I glance down at my outfit—tight khaki shorts and a fitted polo I wore just to needle Jabari—and cringe. *She fits in here. I look like I wandered in from a tourist brochure.*

"Don't worry, girl," she says with a knowing smile that feels like a balm to my bruised ego. "I know the feeling. The men around here will do that to you." The warmth in her tone catches me off guard, but I'm already leaning into it.

"Jade Jackson," she introduces herself, extending a perfectly manicured hand. "Events coordinator. And trust me, I've been managing the Freeman male ego for four years. You'll get no judgment from me."

Her laugh is light and musical, a tinkling sound that loosens the tension in my shoulders. I let out a small, disbelieving chuckle of my own.

"Sierra Watson," I reply, gripping her hand like a lifeline. "And you might just be my new favorite person."

Jade's smile deepens as she wraps me in a quick, unexpected hug. It's warm, genuine, and precisely what I didn't realize I needed.

"Don't worry, I've got you," she says, pulling back. "Jabari told me you'd be shadowing me today. Lucky for you, I've got nothing major on the schedule until later. It's just a wedding rehearsal. How about we grab a coffee at Silver Sands first? You look like you could use a break."

"Make it a coffee with a shot of Bailey's," I mutter, still tasting the bitterness of my earlier clash with Jabari. "If I have to deal with him again, I'm gonna need liquor."

Jade throws her head back and laughs—a full, throaty sound tossed into my spiraling frustration.

"Girl, say less," she says, linking her arm with mine as she leads me toward the golf cart waiting outside.

Moments later, we're zipping across the sprawling grounds of Chesapeake Heights, the breeze teasing my curls and easing the heat of my lingering irritation.

"So, you're a Howard Bison, huh?" Jade teases, her playful tone softening the edges of her usually guarded demeanor. She glances at me, her blue-and-orange Morgan State lapel pin glinting in the sunlight. "Ms. Ann's been raving about you."

I puff out my chest with mock pride. "Yep. And ... you're a Morgan Bear?"

"Guilty as charged," she says with a conspiratorial smile. "You Howard folk always have a way of making yourselves known. Y'all Bougie, right?"

I snort, my aggravation with Jabari momentarily forgotten. "Trust me, there's nothing bougie about Georgia Ave.," I shoot back, thinking of my alma mater's soul-filled streets. "However, we are the Mecca, so being number one comes with the territory. Although in the fifties and sixties, Shaw was where all the Black physicians, lawyers, engineers, and pastors lived. Now, a bit of the soul has been taken out due to gentrification. Plus, a lot of the wealthy Black people I went to school with wouldn't be caught dead living in Shaw. They take their money to Potomac or Kalorama."

Jade chuckles, her laughter mingling with the hum of the cart's engine. "Yeah, once the Obamas moved to Kalorama, that was it." Beneath her playful banter, I detect a guardedness that reflects my own. She holds her secrets, just like I do. So, I steer our conversation back to work.

"So you handle the Freeman male ego, do you?" I inquire, guiding the discussion to shared experiences. "That seems like a full-time commitment."

"You have no idea," Jade says, her smile still touched by

weariness. But her voice has a steely quality, the kind that comes from enduring battles no one else sees.

Something tells me Jade Jackson is more than the resort's events coordinator. She's a quiet force. I deeply admire that because everything about my presence is loud. I'm not complaining because I rock. But it's nice to see another way to do things. Plus, I know working with Jabari, I'm going to need to learn how to woosah before I curse his mean ass out.

"Insufferable, arrogant..." I mutter again, rolling the words around like bitter candy.

"Jabari?" Jade asks knowingly; her raised eyebrow daring me to deny it.

"Who else?" I say, and for the first time all morning, I feel like I'm not alone.

Jade grins, her expression equal parts solidarity and amusement. "Welcome to the club, sis."

And just like that, I know I've found an ally in this place. Someone who gets it. Someone who gets *me*.

* * *

The Silver Sands Café hums with life—a symphony of clinking porcelain, sizzling griddles, and the faint hiss of the espresso machine. The air is rich with the aroma of coffee and the sweetness of caramelized syrup. Jade and I claim a small corner table, its mismatched chairs creaking beneath us like old friends sharing secrets. It's an island of calm amid the bustling chaos.

"Two coffees," Jade orders with a nod, "and add a shot of Bailey's to one of them."

"Make it two shots," I amend, sliding into my chair with a mock glare in her direction. "I have a feeling I'll need the extra courage."

Our laughter is cut short when a woman who introduces herself to me as Marty Jenkins sweeps in like a tropical storm in human form, a tray of drinks precariously balanced in her hands. She's a mass of silver hair and bold colors, and I think I like her.

She doesn't bother waiting for an invitation. Instead, she plops her tray on a nearby table and dives right in, her voice cutting through the ambient chatter.

"Girls! Let's dish," she exclaims, her voice booming over the hum of conversation. For the next fifteen minutes, Marty regales us with Freeman family tales, ending with one about Malik's teenage years. The man was as temperamental as a bull in a china shop.

"He was meaner than a snake with a sunburnt tail," Marty chuckles. "Chased his brother Amir up a tree and left him there for hours!"

Jade's smile falters, and her back straightens. "Malik has always been passionate," she corrects, her voice tight. "But he's also a good man. A very good man. He's just misunderstood."

Marty's eyes sparkle with mischief as she gives us a knowing look. "Oh, I see. Well, I'll catch you two beauties later." She leaves with a flourish, trailing a series of curious glances behind her.

"Ooh, she makes me so mad!" Jade mutters, her cheeks aflame. "Ms. Marty may be sweet, but she's got the subtlety of a sledgehammer."

"Sounds like she just loves stirring the pot," I say, trying to stifle a snicker at Jade's flustered state.

"Trust me, she does," Jade replies, taking a deep breath. "And she does it with everyone."

Her defense of Malik doesn't escape my notice. Leaning forward, I prod gently. "So, you and Malik... You're close, then?"

Jade's smile is bittersweet, a flicker of something deeper dancing behind her eyes. "Let's just say when I needed someone, he was there. He sacrificed more than anyone else would've. I have a little girl, Luna. She adores him, and she's a pretty good judge of character," she laughs. "We like to say he's our bestie. Malik and I, we're just friends."

"Right," I reply, the word drawn out and skeptical. The air between us thickens with unspoken truths. Jade's gratitude toward Malik is palpable yet cloaked in layers of complexity I can't quite unravel.

Plus, Jade's a mom! She didn't mention a father in the picture, but I won't pry. I bet she's fantastic at motherhood; you can tell she's a nurturer.

When our cups arrive, I cradle the warmth, grateful for the liquid courage. We clink our cups, the warmth of the liquor cutting through the tension.

Opting not to pry further, I shift gears. "Well, cheers to friendships, mysterious pasts, and shots of Bailey's before noon."

While we sip, I sense a quiet agreement is taking shape amid our laughter—an alliance in this vast resort under the reign of the Freeman Brothers.

"Any tips on dealing with Jabari?" I blurt out, desperate to steer away from personal landmines and back to the frustratingly handsome thorn in my side.

Jade leans back, her expression thoughtful as she stirs her coffee. "Jabari? Girl, that's a million-dollar question." She sighs, blowing a curl of her bang out her eye. "He's been gone a decade. A Navy SEAL, can you believe it? And some counterterrorism guru or something like that."

"Seriously?" I raise an eyebrow, surprised—the man has more layers than a damn onion.

"His dad was so proud—kept an office for him here at Baycrest, decking it out with all his military shiny things. It's like he always knew Jabari would come back to take over," Jade explains, a note of respect threading her words. "The Freemans are... they've got this tradition, you know? Morehouse men, military service—like a checklist for greatness."

I snort into my coffee. "And let me guess, Jabari's next in line?"

"Right," Jade confirms. "They're protectors, defenders of their legacy and each other."

"Great, just what I need. A control freak with a hero complex," I mutter, taking a swig of my spiked coffee. Then, under my breath, I add, "Does he always have to look so good?"

"Trust me, Ms. Ann makes the finest men on the planet," Jade quips, unaware of the figure approaching us from behind.

"Does she now?" His voice is rich and playful. He steps around to face Jade, and her cheeks bloom the color of ripe cherries.

"Malik Freeman, I'm not stroking your ego today. You know all of you are ridiculously handsome. Women fall over themselves to get a glimpse," she retorts, trying to hide her smile.

So this is Malik? Oh, she may need a shot of Bailey's, too, because this man is all kinds of fine. He's like a more rugged version of Jabari. He has jet-black twists on his head and a five o'clock shadow instead of a beard. But he has those same hazel eyes and a tall, muscular build.

Malik nods, his gaze locking onto hers as he reaches out, fingers gentle as they tilt her chin upward. "That may be so, but I'm only tripping over one jewel in the world's treasure box." His wink is a silent exclamation mark to his flirtatious comment.

"God," I breathe, the air between them crackling with a chemistry so tangible that it's a wonder sparks aren't flying off the duo. Malik's smirk is met with Jade's flustered laughter— the kind that conveys it's laced with nerves, not just amusement.

Then, realizing I'm still at the table, Jade clears her throat.

"Umm, Sierra Watson, meet Malik Freeman," Jade says, tearing her gaze from Malik long enough to introduce us.

Malik's eyes dance with a mischievous light as he takes in my appearance. "Ah, the woman who put Jabari in his place. My brothers Amir and Asa couldn't stop talking about you."

I arch an eyebrow. "And they painted me as what? A dragon lady breathing fire?"

"More like a refreshing breeze on this stifling bay," he chuckles, shaking his head. "Jabari needs to be taken down a peg or two. He thinks he's everyone's boss. You, my dear, are a welcome addition to the team."

"Give him hell," he adds with a wink that suggests he enjoys the idea more than he ought to.

"I'll do my best," I reply, my lips twitching into a smile despite myself. But inside, I'm thinking about how Jabari already has a head start, always one step ahead with those fiery eyes that seem to see right through me. It's infuriating—and a little thrilling.

"Watch out, though, He doesn't play fair." Malik continues, eyeing Jade. "But then again, none of us do."

"Is that so?" I challenge, leaning back in my chair. There's something about Malik's easy confidence that's contagious. Maybe it's the Freeman charm working its magic or the shot of liqueur in my coffee giving me false bravado.

"Yep. We Freemans have our ways," he says, tipping an imaginary hat before striding away, order in hand, leaving a trail of charisma wafting in the air.

"Damn Freemans," I grumble, taking another sip. "Do they offer lessons on how to make women swoon on command?"

Jade catches my words and lets out a laugh, soft and genuine. "Don't worry. You'll eventually figure out how to ignore all that testosterone they sling around. Just give it time."

"Or I could run for the hills while I still can," I joke, but the glint in Jade's eye tells me she knows there's no escaping this—whatever 'this' is.

"Where's the fun in that?" she teases.

"Who said anything about fun?" I reply, but the smirk on my face betrays me. It seems I'm getting sucked into the Freeman vortex. And part of me doesn't want to fight it.

TEN

Killing Me Softly

SIERRA

EVERY DAY, THE TASKS PILE UP, AND SO DOES MY irritation.

The tension between Jabari and me escalates like an unrelenting storm, dark clouds thickening with every interaction. He pushes, and I push back. It's a dance I didn't sign up for, but one I refuse to bow out of.

It's been four days, and his relentless demands, sharp tone, and condescending attitude have grated against my nerves like sandpaper on raw skin. I've dealt with pressure my whole life; it's practically tattooed on my DNA. But Jabari's specific brand of superiority is something else entirely. He speaks to me like I'm beneath him, like I should be grateful for the crumbs of respect he tosses my way.

I know he wasn't thrilled when his mother hired me, but I

chalked that up to the timing—the grief he was still carrying over his father's passing.

But now? I'm starting to believe he has an issue with me. Every word he speaks to me drips with a quiet dismissal. He talks down to me like I'm some obstacle he's forced to deal with instead of a valued part of this team. I can't stand it.

I wish Jade were around to advise me, but she's on vacation for two weeks, so I'm on my own.

I've been around people like Jabari before—people who think their title or family name gives them the right to be smug and dismissive. But it doesn't work for me. I've earned every ounce of respect I've gotten, and I'm not going to let some entitled man-child make me feel small.

But then, there's the other side of him. The side that makes my stomach tighten makes me feel his gaze lingering on me in ways that leave me breathless.

I catch him looking at me, and it's not just an ordinary glance. The look makes my pulse skip a beat like he's seeing something he wants to devour. He's got this intensity, this hunger in his eyes that makes me feel like a deer in headlights.

Tiana swears he likes me and doesn't know how to handle it. I disagree. The man hates me.

He's maddening, and I don't know what to make of him. One minute, he's treating me like I'm invisible—an obstacle in his way—and the next, he's staring at me like I could be something else entirely—something he doesn't want to acknowledge but can't help but want.

I should be more careful. But I refuse to back down.

He doesn't know me. He doesn't know what I've survived. And he sure as hell doesn't get to treat me like this.

Today is no different. We're holed up in his office, drowning in paperwork and unspoken tension. The silence is heavy, charged with the weight of his disapproval. I can feel his eyes on me, watching and judging, but I refuse to look up. I focus on the stack of receipts in front of me, organizing them precisely despite my heart pounding in frustration.

But then I make one small mistake—a simple mix-up of two receipts. And, of course, he seizes on it like a hawk.

"What the hell is this, Watson?" His voice slices through the air, low and razor-sharp.

I stand, walking over to his desk, keeping my expression neutral. It's a tiny error, nothing catastrophic, and I'm ready to fix it. "It's just a mix-up. I'll correct it," I say calmly, hoping to defuse the storm behind his eyes.

But Jabari doesn't let it go. No, that would be too easy.

"Keep up, Watson, or you won't last the week," he snaps. His tone drips with disdain, and then he delivers the actual punch. "I don't know what you're used to in Anacostia, but we work with precision here. You need to respect the level of excellence we demand."

The words hit me like a slap to the face. *Anacostia*. He said it like a curse, like a condemnation.

My neighborhood may not be flawless, but it's my home. It's where I discovered how to endure, battle, and rise up regardless of how tough life knocked me down. And now he stands here, brushing it—and me—aside as if I mean nothing.

My blood boils, and I can feel the tears threatening to rise. But I won't give him that satisfaction. I clench my fists, trying to hold back the fire blazing inside me, but it's useless.

I grab the pitcher of ice water sitting on the desk, and without hesitation, I lift it and pour the entire thing over him.

The shock on his face is priceless. Water cascades down his broad shoulders, soaking his T-shirt and dripping onto the floor. His jaw tightens, his eyes wide with disbelief, and the grumpy mammoth is silent for once.

"What the hell is wrong with you?" he growls, his voice low and dangerous.

"Your disrespectful attitude is what's wrong with me," I fire back, my chest heaving with my anger.

His gaze locks on mine, a storm brewing in his dark eyes, but I don't care.

"In Anacostia," I say, trembling with restrained fury, "respect is earned, Freeman. Not handed out because of a title or a last name."

He opens his mouth, but I hold up a hand, cutting him off.

"You don't know me," I say, maintaining a steady voice. "You lack understanding of my past and my people. If you believe for even a moment that I'll allow you to speak to me as if I were a child, you're completely mistaken."

I pivot on my heel, grabbing my bag as I go for the door. My heart is pounding, adrenaline surging through my veins, but I hold my head high.

My pulse races with a blend of satisfaction and fear. As the door clicks shut behind me, I still feel the weight of Jabari's stare burning into my back, but I don't falter. I refuse to. I've had enough of him—enough of his superiority, enough of the way he seems to think he's the only one with a damn clue about anything.

Watching him out of control for once, drenched and stunned, sent a thrill through me. From what I've gathered, he's always in charge; he's the one who calls the shots and hides behind that cold, calculating mask. But for that fleeting moment, I cracked his stone exterior and saw the man underneath—the one who probably doesn't know what to do with someone like me.

But hell, I'm also picturing the way the water clung to his broad chest and dripped down his hard body, soaking through his shirt. I could count the ridges of his eight-pack abs. He looked like a damn god, even soaking wet and pissed off, his sharp jawline set in that hard line of anger, his dark eyes burning with something that could have been fury or... maybe something else.

No. I don't want to think about that. Not now.

I keep walking, heading for the break room to gather the rest of my things. But before I can get there, the door behind me swings open with a force I can feel through my bones. I don't even flinch.

I hear his voice, low and dangerous, calling my name from behind.

"Sierra!"

I don't even turn around.

As I gather my things, I feel a beat of something else stirring beneath the anger—something darker, more dangerous. It's the way he watches me, the way he keeps trying to peel back my layers. *He has no right.* And damn it, if he wants to know what I'm really about, he'll have to figure it out the hard way.

"Sierra, wait!"

I finally turn, keeping my chin high and maintaining the wall of composure I've spent years perfecting. My hands shake with adrenaline, but I won't show him that. Not now. Not when he's the one who needs to explain himself.

However, when he speaks again, his voice is a mix of frustration and something I can't quite place.

"Have you lost your mind?" he asks. His eyes blaze as he fights to maintain his composure. Water continues to drip from him as his heavy breathing gradually slows.

I narrow my eyes, the challenge in his tone striking me like a shot of whiskey—burning yet sweet in its own way.

"Maybe," I say, my voice steady yet full of bite. "Or maybe you just needed to be put in your place. The world doesn't revolve around you, Jabari. And I may be from Anacostia—"

my voice catches, but I rein in my emotions—"but at least I know how to treat people with common decency and respect."

His jaw tightens, but he says nothing. For a moment, we stand there, locked in some silent standoff, both of us too proud to back down.

I finally break the silence, stepping toward the door again, my hand on the handle.

"I'm done here," I say, my voice as cold as the water I dumped on him. "I quit."

And with that, I walk out.

But as I push through the door and step into the cool air outside, I can't help but feel like the storm's just begun.

ELEVEN
Whatcha Gonna Do

JABARI

She's gone too far. That Siren sent to torment me has crossed a line. She's disrespectful, disobedient—and dangerous.

I'm freezing, drenched in cold water, my anger simmering beneath the surface.

But God help me; I want her more than my next breath.

She can't quit. I forbid it!

I know I went too far with that Anacostia comment. The words slipped out before I could stop them, but I didn't mean it the way she took it. Truth be told, I think she's fantastic. She's resilient and intelligent, and she's already made this place better in less than a week. She took our disorganized employee schedules and turned them into a streamlined machine. Her idea to have my mother give historic walking tours of the resort was brilliant. It's already sold out, and those tours don't start until next week.

We've never had an activities director as well-suited for the job as Sierra. She's made herself invaluable already, and yet, here I am, pissed off and making her life harder.

She thinks I'm a pretentious jackass. Honestly, I'm not sure I care what she thinks of me. But I do care about what she feels about herself. She carries her upbringing like a large chip on her shoulder. I wanted to unsettle her. I tried to put her off-balance the way her mere presence had me. So, I pushed that button.

It was supposed to make her flinch. Instead, it landed harder than I intended. Now, I'm standing here, wet and furious—not just at her, but at myself. I can tell I've hurt her. And damn it, that's the last thing I wanted to do.

I want to apologize to her in the most intimate way possible —with my head between her bewitching thighs, using my tongue and fingers until she's gasping for air and lost in pleasure.

She probably won't be open to that approach—at least not initially.

As I race up the stairs, I run straight into my mother coming down. She looks at my drenched appearance and scowls, shaking her head disapprovingly.

"Jabari Freeman, I don't know what you did or said to Sierra, but you need to fix it. And fix it now!"

I let out a frustrated huff. "Why do you automatically assume this has something to do with Sierra?"

She rolls her eyes. "Son, please. I may be your mother, but I'm not blind. I've seen how you've been pushing that girl all week. It's akin to liking someone and then pulling their pigtails —except you're too stubborn to admit it. I knew something would eventually come to a head between you two. But I never would have guessed it would involve water instead of a punch in the face. Now go fix it - we need her."

With that, she brushes past me without another word, leaving me cursing under my breath as I storm up to my room. Thunder echoes outside, mirroring the storm brewing inside me as I figure out how to make things right with Sierra.

I'll have to find her first.

* * *

After searching the entire resort for over an hour, there is no sign of her, and I'm soaking wet again from the flash rainstorm we just had.

However, she's somewhere on-site because her car is still in the Baycrest driveway.

Now that the storm has cleared out, I find myself standing by the shoreline, the water lapping against the sand, soothing my frayed nerves. I toss a few pebbles into the bay, watching the ripples spread and disappear. The quiet gives me a moment to breathe—something I didn't realize I was missing.

I've been fighting a war inside me ever since Sierra walked into this place, and if I'm honest, I'm not sure how to win it. Whenever I think I've figured her out, she throws me off course. The sharp retort she shot my way this morning—hell, even the way she just stood there and took my anger without backing down—has my mind running in circles. But that's not why I'm here right now. I need space to think, to regroup, because I'm here to do a damn job.

My family expects me to stabilize the resort before I head back to my quiet life on the base, and I'm messing it up by pushing Sierra away.

Sierra Watson isn't my distraction; she's my most valuable employee. I repeat that in my head over and over, hoping it sticks. She's just a part of the team now, and I can't let whatever this... tension is, cloud my judgment or make me lash out.

Then I hear her voice, sharp yet trembling, slicing through the gentle sound of the lapping waves. The piercing sound jolts me from my thoughts, sending a rush through my chest and heightening my protective instincts. She's on the phone, pacing by the water, her free hand tightly clutching her phone as she tosses rocks into the waves, creating ripples that dance across the surface. Each splash feels like a kick to my gut.

I take a step closer, drawn by the urgency in her voice. It's tense, almost desperate, and I can't stop the knot tightening in my stomach.

"Shana, I don't care what you have to say right now!" she shouts, her voice breaking mid-sentence. "You shouldn't have even gotten involved with him in the first place. You knew better!"

Her shoulders shake as she hurls another stone, the splash echoing more forcefully than expected. The way she holds herself, body taut with stress, grabs my attention. Although I shouldn't be listening in, I can't resist—not when her anguish is so palpable, so striking.

"What do you mean they're *coming for you*?" Her voice rises, sharp with panic. "Shana, how much do you owe Dominion? How did it get that high? Do you even hear yourself right now?"

The word hits me like a ton of bricks. *Dominion.*

Damn,. if she's tangled up with them, it changes everything. My mind races, flashing to everything I know all about Jackson Taylor and his crew—their ruthlessness, reach, and bloody reputation. This isn't the kind of trouble you walk away from unscathed.

"I can't just snap my fingers and fix this for you!" she continues, her voice cracking under her frustration. "You got yourself into this mess, and now you're dragging me into it! You —" She stops, cutting herself off with a shaky breath. Then, quieter but no less fierce, she adds, "You always do this, Shana. Always."

I can barely hear the voice on the other end of the line, but I don't need to. The look on her face—the fear in her eyes, the way her jaw tightens as she listens—tells me everything I need to know. Her sister's pleas aren't new. This is a well-worn script, but tonight, it's shredding her.

"Fine. I'll figure something out," she snaps, her tone now hard and clipped. "But don't you dare call me again unless it's with a solution. I mean it, Shana."

She ends the call with a shaky exhale, her shoulders slumping as the fight drains out of her. I take another step forward, my boots crunching softly against the gravel. She whips around at the sound, her wide eyes locking on mine.

"Jabari," she breathes, her voice thick with exhaustion and something close to embarrassment. She tucks her phone into her pocket like she can hide the whole conversation if she tries hard enough.

I don't speak right away, still reeling from what I've just overheard. "Are you okay?" It's a stupid question, one she clearly isn't ready for, but it's all I can manage.

She looks away, shaking her head like she's trying to shake me off. "I'm fine; that was just my sister and I having a disagreement," she says, her voice flat and unconvincing. Then she turns back to the water, her hands curling into fists at her sides.

But I know better. Whatever this is—whatever Dominion has on her and her sister—it's consuming her from the inside. And as much as she tries to shut me out, there's no way I'm letting this go unnoticed.

I want to demand answers, but I know she'll shut me down.

Sierra," I say, my voice laced with concern and determination. "If you ever need to talk, I'm here. I know all about errant siblings. You love them, but they don't always make the best decisions. Then you're expected to clean it up."

She keeps tossing stones into the water, as if she's trying to shut out the world and me. I can't bear to see her like this—so closed off and in pain.

Tell me what's wrong, baby girl. Let me fix it for you.

I take another step closer, careful not to invade her space. But I need to make things right between us. I've been justifying my actions for hours now, but deep down, I know I was wrong to snap at her earlier. And now, with her standing there and the tension between us thicker than ever, I can't keep up the same façade I've worn for so long.

"Look, I..." My words falter for a moment, betraying my usual commanding presence. "That was uncalled for earlier. I'm sorry. I don't know what gets into me when I face off with you. It's like I can't control myself. You drive me crazy."

I expect her to turn, walk away, and completely cut me off. But when she finally meets my gaze, her eyes show no anger. Just a resolute determination that sends a shiver down my spine.

"Apology accepted," she says coolly, but something has shifted between us. Something I can't quite place, but I know it's there.

I breathe, feeling some of the weight of the past few days lift off my shoulders. It's such a relief, but it's not enough. Not yet.

"Thank you," I say, my voice softer than expected. I take her hand in mine, not knowing why I'm doing it—maybe to show her how serious I am or perhaps because I don't want this to be the end of whatever this is between us.

"You're welcome," she exhales. "Do your siblings really do crazy things? You all seem so perfect. You had the perfect life growing up in Chesapeake Heights on the beach, living in Baycrest, having two parents who adored you and a family legacy that carried you."

"Humph," I reply, circling her slowly with my hands behind my back until I stop and face her fully. "Nothing is ever what it seems, Sierra. I'm sure you know that. Did we have a good life? Yes. But it wasn't without problems and impossible expectations. Let's just say a few of us cracked under pressure, and I've had to clean up more messes than I'd like to remember. I may not have been here in the Heights for the past decade, but my siblings knew that I was always just a phone call away. So, we had disagreements, but I always had their back."

I take a chance and reach my hand out to clasp her shoulder. "I'd like to extend that grace to you too. Whatever is causing your face to scrunch up like that." I playfully tip her nose. "You can talk to me about it, and I'll do whatever I can to help."

She looks at me, truly looks at me, with unshed tears in her eyes, and I think she's going to break down and tell me everything. But just as quickly, she puts her mask back on her face and shuts down her emotions.

I remove my hand from her shoulder, knowing the moment's passed.

"Truce," she says firmly, reaching out and gripping my hand with an unyielding strength. And it's not just a truce—it's a challenge. Like she's daring me to do better, to be better to her before she gives me her secrets.

Good Girl.

There's a brief moment when she lightens her grip; testing me, making me prove something to her.

"But don't think your weak-ass apology means you're off the hook, Freeman," she adds, her gaze piercing and unwavering.

I smirk despite myself. That defiance in Sierra keeps me on my toes, constantly pushing me to do better, just like now. "Wouldn't dream of it," I reply with a light tone, trying to ease the tension between us. "As a matter of fact, to show you that I am sorry, why don't you come as my guest to our board meeting tomorrow? My siblings and I are discussing ways to make the resort more profitable. You've had some good ideas already; we could use your spark."

Her face lights up. "Really? You want me there? But I thought you hated my ideas."

I chuckle and shake my head. "No, I only hated that I wasn't the one to come up with them," I admit, turning away from her to throw a rock in the bay. "I'm the oldest son, and now that Papa is gone, this resort—our family, is my responsibility. We can't stay open doing the same old things. I guess you made me feel a little insecure about my place here, whether or not I could do this. I can't leave and return to my life until I do."

She touches my arm, wanting me to look at her, and I do. Maybe I'm imagining it, but she seems pained at my last statement for a second, *like she doesn't want me to leave.* "Jabari, You can do this. You're an amazing leader. I'm an ideas person, but you—you know how to implement and bring a team together. I admire that."

I grin. " Well, I admire your fire, Sierra, and I need you burning next to me tomorrow."

We share a moment of silence, feeling an undeniable pull toward each other that neither of us is ready to admit—perhaps not even to ourselves. The bay gently fades into the background, and I can hear my heart pounding, each beat growing louder with every passing second!

What is this between us? What am I even doing? I'm leaving in a few weeks once everything is settled, and I don't have time to start anything here. But why do I feel the pull to? Do I even still want to leave?

I want to find the answer, but it's not simple. And for the first time, I realize—it doesn't matter. Whatever this is, whatever happens next, I'm not walking away from Sierra Watson or her problem with Dominion.

She has my attention now, and I won't let her get hurt or slip through my fingers.

TWELVE

Do You Know Where You're Going To

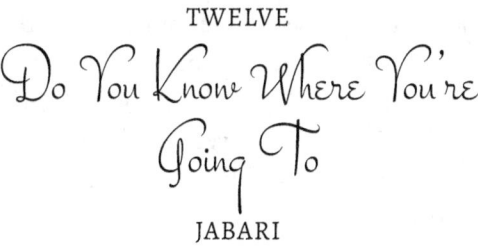

JABARI

UNSURPRISINGLY, OUR FAMILY BOARD MEETING HAS turned into a full-blown shit show.

The weight of the Freeman family legacy is suffocating and unrelenting. The polished wooden table around which we sit is less a place for collaboration and more a battlefield where the future of Chesapeake Heights is being fought over.

I'm thankful Sierra hasn't arrived yet—she'd be mortified by how we're tearing into each other.

I lean forward, planting my elbows heavily on the table, trying to anchor myself in the chaos.

"Listen up," I say, my voice low but sharp enough to cut through the noise. "Every decision we make today will echo for generations. This isn't just about profits or flashy marketing campaigns. It's about preserving the heart of who we are."

Before I can continue, Amir jumps in. As our resident technocrat and cyber genius, he's usually glued to his laptop, but today he's all cocky smirks and easy confidence. His locs are styled into a messy structure atop his head, giving off a casual yet powerful vibe I could never pull off. His designer suit is perfectly tailored to his lean frame, but then he throws me off with the Jordan 11s he paired with it.

I'll never entirely understand my baby brother, but the ladies seem to dig his mysterious yet casual mad-scientist vibe.

"Jabari, you need to chill," he says, waving me off like I'm the dramatic one. "I plan to take this place from the history books to trending on Instagram."

"Instagram?" I repeat, my tone flat, barely masking my irritation.

"Yeah, brother." Amir spreads his arms like he's unveiling a masterpiece only he can see.

"Picture this: hip retreats, exclusive pop-ups, art shows, maybe even some concerts. Millennials and Gen Z? They don't want history lessons—they want vibes."

"Vibes," I echo dryly, my patience already wearing thin. But that's Amir. He might drive me crazy, but I can't deny the spark of creativity that fuels his wild ideas.

"Exactly!" He snaps his fingers, the sound reverberating off the walls, where our ancestors' portraits seem to scowl down at him. "We bring in influencers, throw a few festivals, and boom —Chesapeake Heights becomes the spot everyone's talking about."

"Amir," I say, locking eyes with him, "what you're describing is stripping away everything our great-grandfather built. Dad didn't want this place turned into an event hub for trendy outsiders or the new destination for Bike Week."

"Evolution, big bro," Amir fires back, dismissing my concern with a flick of his wrist. "You can't hold progress hostage in one of your SEAL formations. It's dynamic, like your fancy electric truck."

"Progress doesn't mean selling out who we are," I shoot back, my voice steady but firm.

"Who we are is always evolving," Amir argues, leaning forward now, his eyes lighting up. "It's time we stopped clinging to the past—Negro spirituals and Southern cooking demonstrations—and embraced what's next. Trust me, the younger crowd will eat this up."

"And what happens," I say, a faint, bitter smile tugging at my lips, "when they trample everything in their path?"

"Then we rebuild. Better, stronger," Malik chimes in, jumping on Amir's side with his usual contrarian flair and a grin daring me to shoot him down. He doesn't even agree with him; he wants to disagree with me. "That's what Freemans do, right?"

"We do," I murmur, the words lingering like a challenge and maybe even a threat.

This isn't just a fight about the resort. It's a battle for what the Freeman legacy will mean tomorrow and next year for every generation. And I'll be damned if I let what my ancestors built become another Hilton or Hyatt on the beach with me at the helm. I'd sell it first.

Amara senses the tension building and steps in with her signature grace. "Amir, your vision sparkles, and I can see its promise," she begins, calm but firm, a diplomat at heart. "But stars don't only shine in the new—they're part of constellations, connected by stories that ground us in our history."

Amir leans back, his easygoing smile betraying a flicker of frustration. "You can put all the flowery words you want on it, sis. But History is just that—history," he counters. "Money is slipping through our fingers while we cling to old, dusty memories."

"Memories?" Amara's voice remains steady, but there's steel beneath her words. "Our legacy isn't dust, Amir. It's the soil this resort was built on, rich with the sacrifices and dreams of Freemans who survived far worse than this."

"Storms come and go, sis," Amir shoots back, his grin sharpening into something defiant. "But we either bask in the sunlight after or get left behind in the mud. And let's be real—the way our books look, we're drowning in quicksand. We can't keep catering to these old rich Black families and expect to turn a profit."

"Enough." My voice slices through the room, a command honed by years of leading when emotions ran high. "We're not tossing our heritage aside, and we're not ignoring the winds of change. There must be a middle ground somewhere—a way to honor the past while embracing the future."

Amir huffs. "Here you go with that wise King Solomon BS. Must you always play the peacemaker, Jabari?"

"Peace?" I meet his gaze, unflinching. "This isn't about peace. It's about survival. We can't afford to go all-in on change without anchoring it to what made us strong in the first place."

"Sounds like we're trying to sail in two directions at once," Amara observes, her tone thoughtful as she leans back and swivels in her black leather chair. "Well, if anyone can navigate these waters, it's us."

"Us," I echo, glancing at each of them before letting my eyes drift to the portraits lining the walls. Our ancestors watch silently, their faces etched with pride, resilience, and a hint of challenge. "The Freeman legacy isn't just a relic—it's a living testament. We'll find the balance. We'll chart a course that respects where we came from and drives us toward where we need to go."

"Charting courses now, are we?" Amir teases, his smirk

flashing like lightning, quick and sharp. "Maybe you should captain a cruise ship, big bro."

"Maybe," I reply, a hint of a grin tugging at my lips. "But for now, we focus on steering Chesapeake Heights into a future that keeps it as a beacon—a lighthouse guiding us home, no matter how far the tide takes us."

"Home," Amara repeats softly, her voice an anchor amid the rising waves of disagreement. "That's what it's always been about, not business."

Then, as if summoned by the winds of change we'd been debating, Sierra bursts through the door like a force of nature. Every step she takes toward me at the head of the table is purposeful, her curls bouncing like they're carrying their quiet celebration.

Last night, I had some recon done on Sierra and her sister. I needed to know how deep her sister was in with dominion. It's thirty thousand dollars, and five thousand of that was added yesterday in interest and new debt. Sierra had every right to be pissed at her sister; I'm pissed for her.

I know I crossed a line by invading her privacy, and she'd never forgive me if she found out. It's the only reason I haven't gone to Jackson Taylor and paid the debt myself; Sierra would be livid.

But that doesn't mean I'm not watching the situation closely. Jackson Taylor better not touch one hair on Sierra or her sister's head. And he better not bring that bullshit here to Chesapeake Heights.

I need time to get Sierra to trust me enough to help her. Thankfully, they have a few weeks to pay.

As she walks toward me, she's a vision in another damn wrap dress, but this time it's the same color blue as the Chesapeake Heights Polo she usually wears. The fabric clings to her curves in all the right places, and the soft material accentuates her fantastic figure. Her breasts look good enough to eat, and I can't help but notice how the color makes her freckles stand out like constellations across her skin.

Her presence alone is magnetic, drawing everyone's eyes toward her as she joins us at the table. But when she runs her hand across the back of my neck as she gets to her seat, I have to adjust my erection beneath the table. *I swear, I'm always hard when she's around.*

She slips into the empty seat beside me—because she knows I left it for her—and leans in close, her breath warm against my ear as she whispers, "Sorry I'm late."

I squeeze her hand under the table, a silent reassurance that she's exactly where she needs to be, and pray that my dick calms down before I have to stand up again.

"Good afternoon, everyone," Sierra says, sitting up straight, her voice wrapping the room in a desperately needed warmth. She smiles and confidently places a stack of papers on the table.

"I've been brainstorming some ideas for the resort, and I think these could revitalize Chesapeake Heights."

As Sierra launches into her pitch, I sink back in my chair; arms crossed, my doubts fading with each word. Her ideas aren't merely good—they're revolutionary. For example, she proposes outdoor movie nights showcasing Black filmmakers beneath the county's night sky, cultural festivals celebrating the rich heritage of this land, and adventure trails that intertwine ancient legends with contemporary exploration.

"Imagine," she says, her hands gesturing with a fluidity that paints her vision in the air, "guests reconnecting not just with each other but with the story of this place. We wouldn't just offer relaxation; we'd create memories, anchor people to Chesapeake Heights like it's anchored to us."

Amir jumps up, slapping the table with a loud thwack. "See! That's what I've been saying! People want experiences. How come when I say it, you bite my head off, but when she says it, you're all smiles?"

"Brother, sit down," Asa, his twin, pipes up. His unusual disinterest is replaced with amusement.

I wondered what bothered him today; he's usually the more engaged twin. I'd bet money it has something to do with Raven Ambrose.

"Her plan makes sense, Amir. Yours was all over the place—a bootleg Coachella? Really? Plus, she looks way better than you when she's presenting."

Asa winks at Sierra, and her subsequent blush makes my teeth grind. He knows better than to flirt with my girl.

Wait. My girl? Where the hell did that thought come from?

I force my focus back on Sierra, who continues her pitch with unwavering passion. Her ideas are grounded in a fun practicality that makes even Amir sit down and pay attention. She talks about catering to all ages, ensuring inclusivity, and even securing grants from the state by registering as a historical landmark.

But I'm not just listening to her words anymore. I'm watching her—watching her. The way her eyes brighten with excitement when she talks about possibility. The way her hands move, graceful but firm, emphasizes her conviction.

Despite the walls I've built around myself, her essence seeps through, awakening something inside me that I thought was long dead. After talking with her last night on the beach, something shifted within me, a crack in the fortress I've fortified for years.

Malik leans back in his chair, his eyes gleaming with mischief as he aims a verbal dart at Sierra.

"Your ideas are charming and all," he says, his tone carrying that familiar edge of condescension. "But do you think a few new activities will save us? Especially if we're sticking to our

Black roots. Baby girl, most folks don't care about our history."

Amara stiffens, a suppressed growl escaping her lips despite her usual restraint. She knows what Malik is doing—he pulls the same move on her whenever he wants to assert dominance, cloaked in a thin veil of teasing. My hands tighten into fists under the table, but I don't step in. Sierra can handle this.

And she does.

"Malik," Sierra begins smoothly, her voice calm but firm, her freckles glowing under the light as if they, too, carry a spark of defiance. "Infusing modern charm into your legacy isn't about forcing Black History—our roots—down anyone's throat. It's about inviting others to see its value. Charm, after all, has brought kings to their knees. I think it can help here, too."

Her words glide across the room like a soothing balm, defusing the tension Malik tried to stoke. A faint smile tugs at my lips as I watch her easily navigate his jabs. Sierra radiates a confidence that even Malik can't wholly dismiss.

"Come on now, Sierra," Malik pushes, though his tone has softened, curiosity creeping into his skepticism. "You'll need more than charm and good intentions to convince me."

"Good thing I brought data, then," she counters, her eyes gleaming as she pulls out a stack of documents. "Not just charm."

Her sharp wit earns a chuckle from Asa, who breaks his silence again. "She's got you there, Malik. Plus, let's face it—she also brings beauty."

Sierra blushes again, and I fight the sudden urge to glare at Asa, flirting with Sierra again. I try to force the uninvited jealousy down, but it's not working.

"All right," I interject, steering the conversation back to focus. "Sierra, show us the numbers."

As she spreads charts and graphs across the table, I find

myself drawn to her ideas and her. Not to mention, the numbers look incredible.

"This isn't about chasing trends," she says, her voice threading through the room like a melody. "It's about giving people a reason to connect—with each other, this place, and the history that makes it special."

Malik leans forward now, his reluctance giving way to interest. Amara nods thoughtfully, her analytical mind undoubtedly weighing every point. Asa grins at her like a proud big brother. And even Amir gives her a slow clap.

"Okay," I respond, my voice steady. If we combine these concepts, we can preserve Chesapeake Heights's spirit while embracing your new viewpoint. How can we achieve this without making it a trendy spot that overlooks our history?"

Sierra meets my gaze, her eyes steady and filled with something more profound than determination. "Roots aren't anchors, Jabari. They're lifelines," she says softly. "They don't hold us back; they give us the strength to grow. We create something that lasts by honoring them while embracing the future."

The room falls silent as her words sink in, heavy with meaning. Malik finally leans back, crossing his arms with a reluctant nod. "I feel you, but let's not turn this into a hipster paradise, okay?"

"Noted," she replies, though her focus remains on me.

Seeing my family accept her ideas makes me smile. She's so brave and brilliant. I'm in awe.

As the meeting progresses, her ideas ignite excitement, prompting discussions and even reaching a few agreements. Yet, my mind keeps returning to her. Her suggestion to embrace our historical status is genius, and I know some friends who could assist us in this endeavor.

A few years ago, my team and I helped Chief Adom Annan's brother, Senya, out of a difficult situation in Ghana.

Adom's wife, Maya, is a well-known professor of African Stud-ies. I'm confident she can guide us through the process.

As the meeting concludes, I rise to address the group. "We will proceed with this, but with caution. Any changes we imple-ment must ensure that the Freeman legacy remains robust."

The tension in the room eases, and I feel a glimmer of hope for the first time in weeks.

As the others file out, Sierra lingers, her eyes catching mine. "Thank you," she says softly, her smile a quiet gift, "for giving me a chance."

And momentarily, I forget about the weight of legacy, the burden of leadership. It's just her standing before me, her grati-tude igniting something I didn't realize had gone dark.

"Why don't you thank me properly tonight at dinner?"

Sierra looks surprised, and I hate that. Have I been such an ogre that she's surprised by my dinner invitation?

I smile and grab her hand, caressing her fingers. "Yes, Sierra, dinner. Tonight at Dogon. Let me feed you."

She stares at me, clearly weighing her options before finally nodding in agreement. I kiss her knuckles and let her hand go.

"Good girl. I'll pick you up at eight."

THIRTEEN

Silky Soul

WHY DID I EVER AGREE TO THIS DINNER?

My fingers tremble as they brush the smooth fabric of the emerald dress Tiana has spread out on my bed. Her eyes shine with that 'I told you so' glint. "Girl, this color is going to have Jabari drooling all over himself," she teases, breaking through my wall of nerves with her infectious confidence.

"Can I really pull this off?" I mutter, eyeing my reflection with a mix of hope and doubt. The skater dress seems like a garment conjured from a dream—too luxurious, too vibrant for someone who knows the ebb and flow of Chesapeake Heights better than the high tide of high society.

"Sierra Watson, stop it," Tiana snaps, hands firmly planted on her hips. "You're gonna walk into that restaurant like you own the place because, honey, you could."

I slip into the dress, the satin hugging my curves in a

comforting embrace as if affirming Tiana's words. As I balance on one foot to buckle the gold Louboutin heels, a surge of power courses through me, an electric current from toe to crown. My auburn hair falls sleek and straight around my shoulders, starkly contrasting with the usual wild curls that mirror my free spirit.

"See? What did I tell you? Perfect," Tiana grins, her pride in her handiwork unmistakable.

When Jabari asked me to dinner earlier today, I did not count the cost of saying yes. Dogon is famous African chef Kwame Onwuachi's new DC restaurant. I loved his spot, Kith and Kin on the Wharf, before it closed during the pandemic. He moved to New York after that and has one of the best restaurants in the country, Tatiana; now that he's back in DC inside the famed Black-owned salamander resort, getting a reservation is almost impossible. The fact that Jabari casually mentioned that he was taking me to dinner there tonight was impressive.

I never even tried to get a reservation because the price of a meal there was around four hundred to five hundred dollars, which is not in a school psychologist's salary. So, I jumped at the chance. But once I got in my car and thought about it, I knew I couldn't play. I had to come correct if I was going to Dogon on his arm.

By God's grace, I got my favorite Dominican salon to give me a blowout and silk press in record time. I rarely straighten out my curls, so when I do, it always shocks me when my hair silkily falls to my ass. When the Auburn tresses swing behind me as I walk around, I smile, knowing I look good.

Tiana came over and helped me pick out a dress, and eight outfits later, I finally settled on this emerald-green satin skater dress with the one pair of gold Louboutins I own. I also found the one necklace my sister didn't hawk for her gambling habit that Mama left us, an emerald pendant on a platinum chain with matching emerald studs. Mama came from money, so she always had jewelry and things from her past life, but once she married Daddy, her family cut her off, and we never do that side of the family.

I finished the look by spritzing on some Afrique by Byredo perfume and a little gold body dust. I don't know why this feels like a date, but it's not. This is just my boss taking me to a nice dinner to show his gratitude for helping to turn his resort around. If I keep saying that to myself, I'll believe it, and more importantly, I won't embarrass myself by falling for him.

Jabari is hot and cold. One minute, he's rubbing my arm, holding me steady, and the next, his harsh words push me away. The whiplash is getting old, and tonight, I will enjoy a great dinner and not look too much into it.

When an engine rumbles outside, a deep growl announces Jabari's arrival more effectively than any doorbell could; I'm halfway out the door before Tiana can protest. The cool evening air kisses my cheeks as I step onto the porch.

"Sierra! Wait for him to—" But her voice fades away as Jabari exits his truck, his six-foot-five-inch frame casting a long shadow in the twilight.

"Damn, Sierra, you should've let me come to you," he growls, closing the distance between us with a purposeful stride.

"I can walk ten feet, Jabari. It's not rocket science," I retort, annoyed by the scolding but secretly thrilled by the attention.

"Capable doesn't mean you should have to," he shoots back, his voice a low rumble that vibrates through my core. "You're precious, Sierra. You should be carried every damn step of the way."

His eyes burn into mine, intense and unyielding, and I'm caught—hook, line, and sinker—in their hazel depths, my heart pounding against my ribs like it's trying to escape.

He's rich. And he can be overbearing. But he's nothing like my ex. He sees me, and he appreciates what he sees.

"Sierra, you're so beautiful tonight... it hurts," he breathes out, each word laced with a hunger that sends shivers down my spine.

"Jabari," I whisper, my previous annoyance dissolving into a pool of warmth that pools in my belly. His gaze holds me captive, and I'm suddenly aware of how much I want this man's admiration. How much his approval means to me, despite my best intentions to remain unaffected.

"Let's get you to dinner before I forget my manners and devour you instead," he says, offering his arm with a charm that belies his gruff exterior.

I take his arm, allowing myself to lean into his strength for just a moment—a silent concession that perhaps, just maybe, he's right.

The night air is crisp as Jabari guides me toward the truck, its towering frame casting a shadow across the pavement. "You call this thing a truck?" I can't help but marvel at the hulking machine before us. "Looks more like it's primed for battle."

"Ah, she's not just any truck—this is The Beast." His chuckle rumbles deep in his chest, and I sense a sliver of pride.

"Appropriate," I quip, eyeing the jet-black Ford F-150 with apprehension and awe. "And rather fitting for you, too, I'd say."

"Is that so?" He grins, eyes glinting in the streetlights. "I'll take that as a compliment, Miss Watson."

Before I retort, his hands are on my waist, lifting me effortlessly into the cab. The contact sends an electric shock straight through me, and I gasp. With a wink that should be illegal, he secures the seat belt across me, his fingers grazing my thighs with a touch that sparks fire along my skin. My heart kicks up a notch, betraying my calm exterior.

"Behave yourself, Freeman," I manage to say, though my voice trembles slightly.

"Always," he replies, the corner of his mouth twitching upward before he shuts the door with a solid thud and rounds the truck to get in.

The drive is filled with a comfortable silence, punctuated by the smooth beats of afro-soul and hip-hop flowing from the speakers. I'm surprised; the music doesn't match the man—a closed fortress crafted from duty and discipline.

"Never pegged you for a man who'd appreciate Afro-soul and hip-hop," I admit, turning the volume down a notch. "You always seemed... uptight."

He shoots me a look that has his eyebrow arched in a challenge. "I'm more than you think I am, Sierra. That's exactly why we're doing this dinner. I want to know you, and I want you to know me. We started on the wrong foot, and that's mostly on me."

"Mostly?" I snort, unable to hide the smirk tugging at my lips.

"Okay, Siren," he says, throwing the nickname at me like a gauntlet. "You gave me hell every chance you got."

"Wouldn't have had to if you weren't such a big old grump," I shoot back, folding my arms as I lean against the leather seat. "Being mean was your MO, and I wasn't having any of it."

"True," he concedes with a laugh that shakes the cabin, and for a moment, I see past the façade. There's more to Jabari Freeman than meets the eye, and damn it, I'm starting to want to uncover every layer.

The city lights blur into streaks of gold and silver as we glide through the streets, the hum of "The Black Beast" beneath us a lulling comfort. I can't shake off the sense of anticipation mingling with the faint scent of Jabari's cologne—a woodsy, spiced aroma that feels etched onto my memory.

"Jabari," I start, rolling his name around my tongue like a challenge, "why were you always such a grump around me? It's like you didn't trust me—or anyone else, for that matter."

He let out a sigh, deep and ragged as if he was dredging up ghosts from the very pit of his soul. "I'm only going to say this once because I don't like talking about it." He pauses, jaw clenching. "I used to be carefree and chill, but three tours in Afghanistan can change a man. And coming home to find your fiancée sleeping with your best friend?" His hands tighten on the wheel. "That'll shut your joy down quick."

"Oh my God, that's awful," slips from my lips before I can catch it, an involuntary sound of empathy. "I'm sorry you went through that."

He pulls into the valet spot in front of the Salamander Hotel, DC, the opulence of the place starkly contrasting with the raw vulnerability he'd just shown. "I'm sorry, too. She ended up marrying him, and that's why I don't come home often." There is a shadow in those hazel eyes, something haunted. "She was my high school sweetheart—we had all these plans." A muscle twitches in his cheek. "It hurt, you know? But enough of that sad talk. It's in the past." He turns to me, his gaze softening. "Let's go eat, beautiful."

As I step out of the truck, courtesy of the valet's offered hand, Jabari appears from thin air and pulls me to him with an arm around my waist. He roughly nods at the valet, and it seems he doesn't like the valet touching me.

He's such a possessive caveman, but I kind of like it.

When I think about what Jabari just shared with me in the truck, my mind races, teeming with thoughts of retribution. How could anyone do him dirty like that? He's grumpy but loyal, protective, and has a good heart.

I want to beat her ass, but that's crazy. Imagine me, Sierra Watson, fantasizing about a throwdown at my age. But the thought of someone hurting Jabari, this man—who is, despite all odds, becoming more to me than I dare admit—sparks a fire in my belly that is both terrifying and exhilarating.

"Ready?" Jabari's voice breaks through my thoughts, grounding me as we enter the hotel entrance.

"More than you know," I reply, my words holding a double entendre that even I'm not fully ready to explore.

Stepping into the Salamander Hotel's grand lobby, my breath catches. The opulent chandeliers drip diamonds of light, casting prismatic colors over marble floors so polished, they looked like sheets of ice you could skate across—if you dared. Wealth whispers from the gold-leafed columns to the plush green velvet settees that seem too good for anyone to sit on.

"Damn, Sierra," I mutter under my breath, eyes wide as I drink in the splendor I'd denied myself access to for far too long. It wasn't the lack of funds that kept me away; it was the lack of belief—that someone like me belonged among such finery and deserved to indulge in the fruits of her labor.

Every meticulous detail of this place screams 'exclusive,' and here I am, walking through its doors as if I had every right to be here. Because I do—don't I? The thought feels like a slap—self-inflicted and stinging with truth.

"Beautiful, isn't it?" Jabari's low rumble beside me is a touchstone reminding me that I'm not alone in this luxury ocean. He is the captain of our little ship, navigating these uncharted waters with me.

"More than beautiful," I confess, allowing myself to lean into the awe instead of shying away from it. "I just... I can't believe I've never been here before."

"Sierra," he says, tilting his head, the corner of his mouth lifting ever so slightly, "you work hard in your community. You improve the lives of those kids daily. You should treat yourself like the queen you are, not just when a stubborn man drags you out."

"Drag is a strong word," I shoot back, the words laced with an annoyance that feels like a shield, an armor against the onslaught of emotions threatening to spill over. My heart races with the thrill of being here, with him, and my anger at myself for waiting so long to recognize my worth.

"Strong, but accurate." His chuckle is rich and warm, like a sip of bourbon on a cold night. "You needed a high-handed man to get you here."

"High-handed, huh?" I quirked a brow, matching his amusement with my own. "That's one way to put it."

We stride toward the restaurant entrance, the melodic hum of conversation and clinking cutlery growing louder with each step. The maître d' greets us with a smile that doesn't quite reach his eyes, and I wonder if he sees the invisible marks of 'outsider' stamped on my forehead.

"Reservation for Freeman," Jabari states, his presence demanding attention and respect—not from arrogance, but from a deep-seated confidence that comes from knowing exactly who he is.

"Right this way, Mr. Freeman." We are ushered through the dining area, each table an island of intimacy in a sea of social elegance.

As we settle into our secluded spot, I reflect on Jabari's earlier words about how precious I was to him. This sentiment resonates deep within my bones, a truth I'd danced around, afraid to embrace fully.

"Tonight is the start of that," I whisper, more to myself than to him. From now on, I vow to see myself through Jabari's eyes —a woman worthy of the finest things, not because of what I do for others, but because of who I am. An educator. A counselor. A survivor. And maybe, just maybe, someone's reason to believe in love again.

FOURTEEN

One Hundred Ways

JABARI

WHEN THE WAITER SLIPS AWAY, LEAVING US WITH our menus, I pull a chair for Sierra. Her body is perfection, and I inwardly groan at the way her ass sits up in this dress.

Lord, have mercy.

She sits, her thick hair tumbling over her shoulders, catching the soft candlelight that makes her freckles glow. She's like something out of a dream, all grace and fire, and it takes everything in me not to stare too long.

I slide into the seat across from her, already feeling the pull. She's not just beautiful—she's magnetic. How she holds herself, like she knows exactly who she is and doesn't need anyone's vali- dation, has me hooked. I know she's nervous about being here. This isn't a place she would visit, but the outside world would never know it.

"Thank you," she murmurs, her voice soft as she skims the menu, sneaking a glance at me over the top of the linen paper.

"Thank me? For what? For being completely at your mercy tonight?" I lean back, watching her as her cheeks take on a flush. That blush only makes her more irresistible. "I can't help it, Sierra. You pull me in, and I don't want to fight it anymore."

"Jabari..." Her voice carries a warning, but underneath it, there's something else. Something hesitant but raw. "You don't have to lie to me to kick it. I'm having dinner with you because we're becoming friends and not just reluctant co-workers. Don't try to make me believe it's anything else. I'm not even your type."

"Oh?" I huff. "And what exactly is my type?"

She scrunches her brow and fumbles before saying, "I don't know! But I know it's not a curvy public school psychologist from Southeast DC working on your family's resort for the summer. I'm not from your world."

She's full of shit—literally. I don't know who made this beautiful girl doubt that she's every man's wet dream, but I'm determined to fix it. "Whoever made you question your worth, made you doubt yourself—one day they'll answer to me." The words come out low and fierce, hanging between us. I do not make empty promises, and I hope she knows that.

"Let's not go there," she says, but her hand twitches on the table, giving her away. Before she can pull it back, I cover it with mine.

Her skin is soft, her touch electric. "Thank you for being here tonight," I say, meaning every word. "You've made me feel like the luckiest man in this room."

"Jabari, you're laying it on a little thick," she says, though her eyes sparkle. She likes it—she can't hide that, and honestly, I don't want her to.

"Maybe. But you're worth it," I tease, my voice dropping lower.

Her laugh is soft, almost shy, and I swear it's the sweetest sound I've heard all week. She drops her menu and lets out a frustrated sigh. "Okay, I give up; how do we order off this menu? There are too many small sections."

I chuckle and lift my menu between us, my eyes meeting hers over the edge. "This is how it works," I say, letting my voice drop to that rumble I know gets to her. "It's a tasting menu. We pick a bunch of things to share."

"Share?" She raises an eyebrow, a flicker of surprise flashing in her eyes. "You and—we're going to share food?"

"Absolutely," I say, grinning. "Tonight, I'm going to feed you." The words roll off my tongue smooth as silk, and I don't miss how her breath catches.

"I may love to eat, Jabari," she says, leaning in just enough for her voice to wrap around me, "But I'm a picky eater. And this is a lot."

"Trust me, you'll savor every bite." I know she's thinking about the cost—practical to a fault—but that's not her problem tonight. She's with me, and when you're with me, you don't worry about a damn thing.

The waiter returns, and I rattle off our order: coco bread, cornbread, lamb, shrimp with a kick, lobster, and a plate of jollof rice and chicken. It's comfort food—my food.

"Jabari, are you sure—" she starts, but I cut her off with a wink.

"Relax. I've got this."

Dinner becomes its own kind of game. The air shifts, the tension turning warm and playful as she laughs at my jokes and throws back quick comebacks. I insist on feeding her—a piece of lamb here, a forkful of rice there. She fights it at first, her independence flashing in those eyes, but eventually, she softens.

Every time my fingers brush her lips, her body relaxes more. Every flick of her tongue, every quiet sigh, tightens something deep inside me. And if my pants get any tighter, my dick is going to bust through.

"Stop it," she says, but her voice is weak, her protest half-hearted when I lick a dollop of butter that fell to her fingers.

"Can't." My voice is rougher now because this woman is doing things to me I can't ignore.

"Jabari..." Her tone shifts, and there's no mistaking the heat simmering in her words.

"Sierra." I hold her gaze, daring her to admit what's building between us. She doesn't, but she doesn't have to. It's all there, written in how her lips part and her body leans just a little closer to mine.

The moment is interrupted when the waiter drops the check on the table, but Sierra moves fast, her hand darting out like lightning to grab it.

"Sierra," I warn, my voice steady but low. "Don't even think about it."

"It's just a check, Jabari," she says, feigning innocence, but the spark in her eyes gives her away.

"Touch it, and I'll take you over my knee right here," I say, my voice dropping to a growl. "Spank you until you're a real redbone."

She gasps, her cheeks flushing that perfect shade of pink. "You wouldn't dare."

"Try me," I shoot back, my jaw tightening as I dare her to test me.

Her hand retreats, and she pouts, crossing her arms with a defiance that only makes me want her more.

"Good girl," I say, my voice softer but no less firm. It's not a dig—it's appreciation. This woman is fire, and I want to get burned.

I stand, holding out my hand. For a moment, she hesitates, but then her fingers slide against mine, and it feels like victory.

"Come on, Siren," I say, my voice coaxing. "Let's return to Chesapeake Heights and walk by the water."

"Jabari, I live here in the city; that's almost an hour away. Are you going to want to bring me back home?"

"No, but I will," I say with a wink. "Plus, it's Friday night. We've got nothing but time."

"Okay," she relents, "but you're bringing me home. I'm not staying at Baycrest tonight."

"Noted." I nod and squeeze her hand.

We leave the restaurant, stepping into the cool night air, the city stretched before us, the path ahead shimmering with promise. Whatever is between us, it's not going away—not tonight, maybe not ever.

When we return to Baycrest and step outside, the salty air greets us like an old friend. The bay glimmers in the fading sunlight, its surface alive with soft ripples. The boardwalk stretches ahead, quiet and calm, a perfect backdrop for the storm brewing between us.

"You know," I say, breaking the silence as we walk, "Chesapeake Heights isn't just land or buildings to me. It's blood, sweat, and generations of dreams. People who dared to think beyond their reality. That's why I fight hard to hold on to our roots, even as we grow. And I'm grateful you helped me figure out how to do both."

Sierra glances at me, her eyes warm and thoughtful, reflecting the golden hues of the setting sun. "I can see that, Jabari. It's clear how much this place means to you. Your commitment to your family's legacy—it's part of what makes you... you."

Her words, simple but sincere, settle over me like a balm.

"Exactly," I say, my voice softer now. "But what about you, Sierra? What drives you to pour yourself into helping others?"

For a moment, she hesitates. Then, her voice wavers as she opens up like she's stepping into uncharted waters. "When I lost my mom, everything fell apart. It was... chaos. Like being unmoored in a storm." She swallows, steadying herself. "Shana —my sister—she carried the weight of it all. She gave up everything to make sure I was okay. It wasn't all roses; at one point, she became an alcoholic. But she went to court-ordered rehab and has been sober for six years now. But then she met a trifling character and got into gambling. I believe she's trying to piece her life back together, and I just... I owe her. She kept me when she didn't have to.

Her words hit me like a punch to the gut. The pieces click together: her fire, her drive, the desperation I caught in her voice when she argued on the phone about Dominion. It all comes back to taking care of her family. Just like me.

"You're resilient," I say before I can stop myself.

Her gaze meets mine, and she smiles, a little sad and proud. "Exactly," she echoes, and I see the strength behind her vulnerability for the first time. "And now, as a counselor, I get to be part of someone else's survival story. Maybe offer them the same stubborn hope that got me through."

"Stubborn hope," I repeat, the phrase settling into my chest, warm and familiar as it belongs there.

"Jabari," she asks, her voice softer now, more tentative. "Can I ask you something?"

"Anything."

"Why do you call me Siren? It feels... loaded. And if I remember correctly, Sirens from Homer's *Odyssey* weren't exactly nice."

I stop walking and turn toward her, closing the space between us. My hands itch to touch her, so I tuck them into my pockets. "No, they weren't," I say, my voice low. "But they were beautiful, mesmerizing. They had this pull, this power no one could resist. You, Sierra, have had me under your spell since you cursed me out for canceling your interview."

She gasps and smacks my arm, her laughter cutting through the moment's weight. "Jabari Freeman, you know I didn't know your daddy had passed. I didn't even know you existed."

I laugh, shaking my head. "No, you didn't. But that didn't stop you from telling me to go to hell."

Her hand slips into mine, a quiet truce. "Yeah, well, my temper gets the best of me sometimes," she says, her tone soft but teasing.

"Good," I say, leading us forward again, our steps falling into sync. "I like your fire."

She studies me as I glance toward the bay, letting the view ground me. "For someone who's seen the world, you've got this look like everything here is brand new to you," she says, her smile teasing but warm.

"Maybe it is," I admit, the confession leaving me raw. "New and terrifying."

"Good terrifying or bad terrifying?" she asks, her voice light, but her eyes dig deeper, peeling back layers I've worked hard to keep in place.

"Is there such a thing as good terrifying?" I try to deflect, but the words don't hold their usual weight.

"Absolutely," she says, her fingers brushing against mine, setting off a chain reaction I can't ignore. "It's the terror that reminds you you're alive. That you're capable of feeling something other than duty, and it reminds you that you need God."

The truth in her words pins me in place. I pull her closer, the golden light bathing her in a glow that makes her look like she belongs to the sunset.

"Sierra—" Her name catches in my throat, weighted with everything I want to say but don't know how.

She steps closer, her hand tightening around mine. "Jabari, if you don't kiss me right now, I swear I will do something drastic."

Her boldness breaks the last thread of my restraint. I don't think. I act, closing the distance between us in a heartbeat.

Everything I've held back when our lips meet explodes— desire, hope, fear. It all pours out in the kiss, raw and unfiltered. Her hands find my shoulders, grounding me as I pour myself into her. Her taste is sweet and addictive.

When we finally pull back, her breath mingling with mine, she grins up at me, her eyes sparkling like the bay.

"Joy looks good on you, Jabari," she whispers, her voice carrying a warmth that seeps into every part of me.

And just like that, I know—I'm a goner.

She's mine, and nothing will keep me from her.

FIFTEEN

The Way I Want To Touch You

JABARI

I WAKE UP ALONE.

The sheets beside me are cold and untouched as if the emotional and physical connection Sierra and I made last night never happened.

She didn't come home with me, but she wanted me. That was evident in every extra second she took to leave my side.

I wanted her, too.

I sit up, running a hand over my face, trying to shake off the weight of uncertainty on my chest. The morning sun filters through the sheer curtains, casting golden streaks across the room, but I don't feel its warmth. Not yet. Not until I figure out what's going on with me.

I've spent years mastering my emotions, every reaction, every feeling, and every vulnerability that could be taken advantage of. That kind of discipline was instilled in me during my time in the SEALs, reinforced by my father's high expectations, and firmly locked away when Vee walked away from our relationship without a glance back.

And yet, here I am, waking up thinking about a woman who shouldn't have this kind of hold on me.

Sierra.

She's everywhere.

Her laugh lingers in my head like a favorite song. Her scent —vanilla and something subtly sweet—still clings to my skin. I can still feel the way she fit against me by the beach, how she moaned through that kiss like I was the only man who had ever touched her the right way.

Fuck.

I shouldn't be feeling like this. I shouldn't be wanting her this much.

But I do. And it terrifies me.

Because the last time I allowed someone in—when I let a woman mean something to me—I lost more than just love. I lost myself.

Vee didn't merely betray me; she shattered everything I believed about loyalty, trust, and what it meant to be chosen. I was prepared to build a future with her, and she walked away as if it were nothing as if *I* were nothing.

I swore I'd never put myself in that position again. I'd never let another woman get under my skin like she did.

And yet, Sierra...

She makes me forget all my reasons for keeping my walls up. She doesn't try to impress me, hold back her opinions, or shrink herself to fit into anyone's world. She challenges me and makes me laugh, and for the first time in a long while, I feel like I can breathe with her.

And that's dangerous because she could undo me if I'm not careful. She could become something real, something permanent. And there's nothing permanent about my life right now. I don't know if I'm staying in the Heights to lead the family business fully or if I'll hire a manager and return to my life in VA Beach.

I exhale and push to my feet. The wood floors are cool against my bare skin as I move toward the window, which overlooks the sprawling Chesapeake Heights Beach Resort.

The waves roll lazily in the distance, like last night when I kissed her under the stars.

I can still feel the ghost of her lips on mine and taste the remnants of honey and wine on her tongue. Last night, under the moonlit sky, she unraveled me—slow and sweet, yet dangerously potent. That kiss wasn't just a kiss; it was a promise. And damn, if I don't plan on collecting.

And just like that, my dick hardens again.

I need to see her.

I need to know that this isn't just in my head, that she feels this too—that I'm not alone in this madness.

I grab my phone from the nightstand, my thumb hovering over her number.

She wouldn't usually work on Saturdays, but she's covering for Jade today while on vacation. Looking at the clock, I see it's 9:00 am, which means she's likely already on the property.

No need to call when I can touch her.

For the first time in years, I feel like a man on the edge of something he can't control.

Because Sierra Watson isn't just a distraction, she's a threat.

Not to my safety. Not to my reputation. But to the one thing I swore I'd never risk again.

My heart.

I quickly move through my morning routine—shower,

jeans, fitted tee, boots. I don't have time to waste. There's only one thing on my mind.

Find Sierra.

The resort is already waking, but the usual morning chatter —staff prepping for events, tourists meandering toward the beach—barely registers. I scan the grounds until I spot her standing outside the stables, hands perched on her hips, her gaze locked on the horses.

She's breathtaking.

The morning breeze plays with the hem of her white sundress, shaping the soft fabric against her curves. There's a wedding later this evening, and I believe she's helping fill in for Jade since she's still on vacation. That explains her attire. Auburn curls cascade over her shoulders, catching the sunlight and glowing like embers. When she bites her lip, a spark ignites in my chest.

Damn, I want her again.

I step up behind her, my voice a low rumble. "What are you doing hiding out by the barns, *Siren*? You'll get yourself dirty."

She smirks but doesn't turn. "I was thinking about a handsome man who gave me an incredible kiss after a fascinating dinner."

I chuckle, stepping closer, my heat pressing into her back. "Oh?" I murmur, my lips just near her ear. "And what about this handsome man? Will he have the chance to feed and kiss you again?"

She inhales sharply. "God, I hope so," she whispers.

I don't hesitate.

I turn her in my arms, gripping the nape of her neck as I claim her mouth. She parts for me instantly, melting against my chest as our tongues tangle. Her moan vibrates between us, sending a charge straight through me.

She tastes like sugar and something purely Sierra—sweet, wild, and utterly addictive.

I could kiss her all day, but I pull back, resting my forehead against hers.

"Come ride with me."

She blinks, lips swollen, eyes heavy. "What? Ride... what?"

"The horses," I say, brushing my thumb over her lip and smirking. "Have you ever ridden before?"

She shakes her head, looking back at them. "No, but they're beautiful. I wish I could."

I glance at the five Black Quarter Horses standing proudly in their stalls. As I stroke their manes, I nod to each one, "Zeus, Athena, Hermes, Aphrodite, and Hades."Her brow lifts. "Greek mythology, huh?"

I laugh. "My father was obsessed. Thought they sounded *majestic.*"

"I like it." She steps toward Zeus, the largest and gentlest. He's also the oldest and my mother's favorite horse. Of course, Sierra would be drawn to him.

"Do you want to ride him?"

Her lips part, hesitation flashing across her face. "I don't know if I should. I'm not experienced at all."

I slide behind her, my hands skimming her waist. "I'll teach you." My voice is coaxing, laced with promise. "I won't let you fall."

She exhales, then nods.

"Alright, Freeman. Show me how to ride."

Fifteen minutes later, Sierra is perched on Zeus, gripping the reins tightly with both hands. Although her dress will be messy by the end, she seems to have forgotten why that matters. I haven't forgotten, though. I've already texted Amara to find her another dress.

"Relax," I tell her, adjusting her grip. My hands linger on hers, my touch deliberate. "Zeus can feel your nerves. Just breathe and trust me."

She exhales and settles into the saddle, but tension still lingers in her shoulders.

Damn, she's stunning. Her thighs hug the saddle, her dress draped across her legs, her back straight, looking every bit like a goddess mounted atop a beast.

"Alright, let's move." I swing onto Hades beside her, keeping a slow pace as we ease onto the trail.

The sun warms our skin as we move beneath the arching trees. Oak leaves sway overhead, dappling golden light along the winding path. The salty breeze carries the scent of cedar and earth, mingling with the quiet sound of hooves pressing into damp soil.

We discuss the resort and the revitalization of Chesapeake Heights. Her passion and ambition are evident, and I admire her sharp mind and abundance of ideas.

But I also admire how she releases her fear with each step, leans into the ride, and lets her laughter echo through the trees like music.

Then, I nudge Hades into a faster pace. Zeus instinctively follows, and Sierra lets out a surprised yelp before laughter overtakes her.

"This is *amazing!*" she calls, gripping the reins tighter, her curls whipping behind her.

"You look good up there, Watson," I smirk, watching her move with the rhythm of the ride.

We gallop for a while, the world blurring into a rush of speed, wind, and adrenaline. Her eyes are wild with exhilaration when we slow again, and her breath is ragged.

"That was incredible," she pants, looking at me with something raw and unguarded. She jumps down with my assistance and kisses the side of Zeus' face, whispering. "I want to ride you every day."

Lucky Bastard.

We walk back to the barn so I can show her how to properly tack and care for the horses before and after a ride. But she throws herself into my arms before I can begin my lesson.

And just like that, the lesson shifts.

Her breath fans against my jaw, her fingers gripping my shoulders. "Thank you for this," she whispers.

I can't wait any longer.

I crush my mouth to hers, kissing her deep, my hands fisting into her hair. She moans, pressing tighter against me, her body molded to mine.

Her hands are everywhere. Caressing the muscles and hard lines, I've spent the past decade crafting. When she runs her hand over my erection, I hear a slight moan in the back of her throat, and I bite her lip.

She returns my gesture with a hard squeeze of my dick, and I swear I'm about to blow my load inside this barn.

I tear my lips from hers and hold her back by her shoulders, breathing heavily. "Watch it, baby girl. If you touch it, you own it."

The Siren smirks and squeezes my dick with even more pressure, making me groan.

Then, she wrecks me.

She drops to her knees.

Fuck.

"Sierra," I rasp, stepping back. My fingers dig into the wooden stall holding Aphrodite, and Sierra looks up, her eyes dark with hunger.

"I want to taste you," she breathes.

I curse as she unzips my jeans, freeing me with agonizing slowness. The second her warm mouth wraps around me; my head falls back.

Jesus fucking Christ.

Her lips glide down my hard dick, her soft tongue swirling, teasing. My hands tangle in her curls, gripping but not forcing.

She sets the pace.

She's in control.

One hand strokes while her wet mouth works me like she was born for this.

Her pretty red nails dig into my thighs, and when she moans around me, the vibration makes my knees buckle.

"Damn it, Sierra," I groan, my abs tightening, every muscle coiling with pressure.

She hums, the sound sinfully sweet. Her eyes are locked on mine, her pupils blown wide, completely undone by this.

She's getting off on this.

The knowledge sends a raw thrill through me.

Her rhythm increases, her cheeks hollowing, her throat taking me deeper. My grip tightens in her hair, my control fraying.

"Fuck—" My voice is wrecked, my body trembling.

She slides her hands between her thighs and jerks to her finish.

And that's it. I'm gone.

My release hits like a lightning strike, tearing through me as I spill into her mouth, groaning her name like a prayer.

She swallows every drop, her tongue flicking over me once more before she leans back, licking her lips.

I drag her up, kissing her fiercely, tasting myself on her tongue.

"You're going to be the death of me," I murmur, breathless, shaking.

She smirks, her fingers still gripping my waist. "And your sinful taste will ruin me, Jabari Freeman."

I chuckle, gripping her chin, pressing a slow, lingering kiss to her lips.

I'll never get enough of this woman.

SIXTEEN

Human Nature

I CAN'T BELIEVE I SUCKED JABARI OFF IN A BARN.

Hell, just last week, I walked away from Jabari with a smile on my lips, savoring the rare victory of getting that jackass to apologize.

I couldn't help but feel a little smug about it. It's not every day you manage to crack the impenetrable fortress that is Jabari Freeman.

Then, a day later, I walked out of his family board meeting with the biggest win yet and managed to impress him.

Yesterday, we had dinner and a kiss that lit my soul. I don't know what any of it means, but I know one thing-I've conquered Jabari Freeman.

If this past week has taught me nothing else, it's taught me that Jabari thrives on being right, and no matter how convincing your argument, it's nearly impossible to make him see any other perspective but his own.

On my second day on the job, I casually suggested to Jabari that a historic walking tour with Ms. Ann as the star could be a real crowd-pleaser for our visitors. I still remember the chill when his eyes flicked to mine—sharp, calculating, like I'd just proposed throwing a naked orgy on the beach. His jaw clenched, his body tensed for battle.

"No," he snapped, his voice tight with annoyance. "That's not happening. We don't do things like that here. My mother is not for sale, and neither is our history."

I raised an eyebrow, fighting the urge to smirk. I should've known. Jabari was a man who liked to dictate the pace. But I didn't back down. His reaction was exactly what I expected, but it still left me wondering—how could someone dismiss an idea so quickly without even considering it?

Undeterred, I spent the next hour working the crowd, pitching the idea to anyone who'd listen. By the end of it, I had over a hundred sign-ups. I was practically walking on air as I marched back to Jabari, confident that he'd have to admit I was right this time. But when I presented my results, instead of the praise I'd imagined, he sighed again—a deep, long-suffering sound that was practically a grunt—and turned on his heel, storming off in the opposite direction.

It stung a little, but honestly? It just fueled my resolve. Every chance I got, I proved Jabari Freeman wrong.

When he called my historic tours brilliant during the apology he offered yesterday, that was the icing on the cake. Sure, it wasn't the most heartfelt of apologies, but it was a concession, nonetheless. A rare one. And that made it feel like a victory, the kind I could savor while I tried to wrap my head around how my heart had gone this far for him.

I'm craving a man I know isn't free to love me.

Even if Jabari wasn't an arrogant jackass or my boss, he's leaving. He's made it abundantly clear that once the resort is stable, he's heading back to his life in VA. Beach. I won't volunteer for the heartbreak I know would ensue by acting on this crazy infatuation between us.

It's Sunday, and I finally have a day off. Covering for Jade was incredible; I love weddings. But I'm exhausted.

I feel on top of the world after dinner, the trail ride, and that incredible kiss with Jabari. I won't even get started on the head I gave him; I swear I came just as hard as he did. I should be on cloud nine right now. But I still can't shake the memory of my last conversation with my sister. The one where Jabari caught me on the beach before he apologized.

I pray he didn't overhear too much—especially about Shana and her mess. The last thing I need is for Jabari, or anyone in his family, to know why I'm working at Chesapeake Heights. If they find out about my sister's debts, Dominion, and everything else, I'll be out the door before I can blink.

Jabari protects his family at all costs, attraction to me and my ideas be damned.

Shana's troubles are my albatross, my cross to bear. She has always struggled with addiction, and when I was still in high school, she spiraled into alcoholism. I'd come home to find her passed out, surrounded by empty bottles and the smell of regret. But the most challenging part came after Mom passed. Shana couldn't cope, and when she got her second DUI, they sent her off to rehab.

For a while, it worked. She came out sober, but it wasn't long before the gambling started. The slots and sports betting were initially harmless, or so I thought. Then she got involved with Dominion private rooms, and before I knew it, I was bailing her out of debt again. Only this time, it wasn't just her. It was everything. Our family home, her car, and even most of the jewelry our mom had left us. I've repeatedly paid her debts, but this time is different.

I am done enabling her. I can't do this forever. I have my own life to live, but I'm tied to her, her addiction, her mess. The hardest thing is knowing I can't just walk away. She's my sister, and I promised Mom I'd always care for her.

When Shana called a few days ago, hysterical and paranoid, convinced she was being followed, I hesitated to go to her. I knew what was happening—she was broke, hiding her losses. She needed me to top her bank account and probably some food. I took the $5,000 she had on her last week for safekeeping and hoped she'd stay out of trouble. But she still has a job at a local bar, and I'm sure all her tips are returning to a gaming table.

But here I am, pulling up to her apartment complex off Benning Road, knowing exactly what's waiting on the other side of that door—Shana, begging and pleading for money I don't have. The thought twists in my stomach, but it's nothing compared to the sharp sense of unease prickling at my skin. The parking lot is too quiet, the kind of quiet that feels unnatural. My steps falter as I glance around, clutching my bag tighter against my side.

The hairs on my neck stand up a second before it happens.

A hand grabs me hard, yanking me backward with enough force to knock the breath out of me. My phone slips from my fingers, skidding across the pavement as I let out a strangled scream.

"Sierra Watson," Jackson Taylor purrs, dragging me around the corner into the shadows. His grip is like iron, and he only tightens his hold when I try to pull away. "You're a hard woman to find these days. But I knew you'd show up here eventually. You always do."

My pulse pounds in my ears, fear swallowing my voice whole. I thrash against him, but it's no use. He slams my back against the cold brick wall, his face close enough that I can see the sick satisfaction gleaming in his dark eyes.

"Two more weeks," he says, his lips curling into a cruel smirk. His free hand brushes against my arm, sliding lower, and I freeze. "That's all you've got. Unless, of course..." His hand trails to my hip, lingering there as his voice drops, taunting. "You'd rather settle this another way. A couple of nights in bed with me, and I'll forget this whole little debt of your sisters. I've already had her; I want you to. I like to complete my collections.."

The words are like a slap, and a surge of anger cuts through my fear. "Get your hands off me, Jackson," I spit, my voice shaking but firm.

"Oh, Sierra," he says, chuckling as he presses closer. "Still so fiery. It's almost a shame you're wasting all that energy working that second job for your sister. You should be thanking me for giving you an out. On your back."

The weight of his body pins me to the wall, and panic claws at my throat. He smells like expensive cologne and bourbon, which makes my stomach churn. I twist my body, shoving at him with all my strength, but it's like trying to move a brick wall.

"You're not going anywhere until I say so," he sneers, his hand sliding down my thigh.

That's when something in me snaps. I won't let him control me—not now, not ever. My knee shoots up before I even think, connecting with his stomach. The impact forces a guttural grunt from him, and for a split second, his grip loosens.

I shove past him, my breath coming in ragged gasps as I sprint toward the stairs. Behind me, his laughter echoes, sharp and mocking.

"Run, Sierra! Run while you can!" he calls, his voice following me like a shadow. "But remember—two weeks! Tick-tock, baby."

I don't stop until I'm pounding on Shana's apartment door, my chest heaving and tears threatening to spill. The weight of what just happened presses down on me, but I shove it aside. I can't afford to break down. Not here. Not now.

I might be terrified, but I'll be damned if I let him win.

I knock, but there is no answer. I knock again. Silence. I called her thirty minutes ago, and she said she'd be home waiting for me. Panic begins creeping in. This isn't like her. She's generally where she thinks she'll be, especially if she needs money.

I push open the door using the spare key she gave me when she moved in. Slamming the door shut and locking it, my hands still shake as I lean against it, my mind racing. I call her name and look towards the kitchen.

Then my heart drops.

The sight before me is something I've feared but hoped would never come. Shana is sprawled on the floor, surrounded by broken glass and overturned furniture. Her face is battered and swollen, and blood is caked at the corner of her mouth.

I rush to her side, fear and sadness colliding in my chest as I try to comfort her.

"Shana, oh my God, what did he do to you?" My voice cracks, emotions thickening the air between us.

She stirs weakly, barely able to focus on me. "He... he came for me, Sierra..." Her voice was barely a whisper, but her words hit me like a freight train. "Jackson... He said I had two more weeks. This was... motivation." She winces with each word, pain radiating from her broken body.

"Shhh, it's going to be OK. Let me call the police."

But she grabs my hand with surprising strength. "No, Sierra, no police... No hospitals. He'll kill me if the cops get involved."

I blow out a frustrated breath, knowing she's right. Her life is in danger, but so is mine if I call the cops on the Jackson Taylor. As I observe her arm hanging limply at an odd angle to the side and blood soaking through her clothes, I know there was only one place I can take her—Chesapeake Heights Resort.

The resort has a fully staffed, private, 24-hour urgent care center. No one who worked there would say a thing about treating her. The doctors and nurses are used to keeping the medical emergencies of rich Black folk quiet. I wouldn't be surprised if there were a Diddy party element within the summer crowd: baby Oil, orgies, and old men popping Viagra to participate.

To get access to the clinic, I need permission. I don't have that kind of pull. And calling Jabari? That's a whole other question. I know Ms. Ann will help, but she has her burdens. Yesterday, I caught her sobbing by an old oak tree during lunch. She called her husband's name repeatedly while punching the tree trunk, and I watched from afar to ensure she didn't hurt herself. She's not handling the death of her husband as well as her kids think she is. But it's not my place to say anything.

Jabari won't just want to help—he'll want answers. And I'm not ready to give them. This is my mess, and I refuse to drag him or his family into it.

Still, I can't stand here any longer, staring at my sister, knowing she needs my help. If he's the only one who can give it, so be it. I have to get her to my car and pray she can stay stable enough for the hour-long drive into Calvert County.

Pulling my phone out, I take a deep breath and make a call that I know will change everything.

He answers on the first ring, like he was waiting for me.

Maybe he was.

"Sierra?" The tenderness in his voice is my undoing, and my heart cracks open right then and there.

"Jabari," I cry out between sobs. "I need you."

SEVENTEEN

You Should Be Mine

JABARI

I'M PACING THE CLINIC WAITING ROOM LIKE A panther, coiled and ready to strike. Every step echoes the chaos inside me, my chest tight with tension I don't know how to name.

When Sierra's name lit up my phone, my heart jumped like it was wired to hers. I'd just left her yesterday—in that barn, under an orgasm-induced haze heavy with hope—but hearing her voice now, broken and desperate, flipped something inside me.

The protector reserved for my sister and mother clawed its way to the surface, and I swear, whoever made Sierra Watson cry like that won't get away unscathed.

Nah. Not while I'm breathing.

I don't make it a habit to fight for anyone who isn't blood. My ex-fiancée, Vee, saw to that. She didn't just break me when she left; she hollowed me out and left me a shell of the man I used to be. But Sierra? She's something else entirely. Light and fire wrapped in this freckled, honey-dipped package that feels like a second chance I never saw coming.

And now her sister's hurt. Hurt bad enough for Sierra to bring her here, needing privacy and safety she doesn't trust anyone else to provide. She didn't have to explain. I didn't ask questions. I knew she wasn't in any state to answer them. Whatever she needed, I'd make it happen.

I'd shift the sun and the moon for her if she asked.

Still, I'm no fool. Jackson Taylor's name hovers like a shadow over this whole mess. She didn't say it, but I don't need her to. My gut tells me he's behind it—the debts, the threats, the danger circling her family like vultures.

The second she hung up, my SEAL instincts kicked in. Within minutes, I'd tracked every breadcrumb that led back to him.

Now, I'm on the phone with Jackson, holding my temper in check as his slimy voice slides through the receiver. He's trying to sound confident and push some weak-ass negotiation like he doesn't already know he's playing with fire.

"You've got some fine taste, Freeman," Jackson drawls, his tone oozing with mockery. "That employee of yours? Damn shame I didn't know she was yours from the start. If I had..." He chuckles, low and taunting. "Let's just say I'd have kept my hands to myself. Probably."

My grip on the phone tightens, and every muscle in my body is restrained. He's trying to bait me, testing my limits like the fool he is. But I let him talk, the silence on my end louder than any threat I could make.

"She's a fine piece of ass, though," he continues, his voice dipping like he's savoring the words. "Got a real fight in her, too. I like that. But don't worry, Freeman. I didn't do anything... permanent." He laughs again, and the sound ignites a fire in my chest.

"Listen to me, Jackson," I growl, my voice low and lethal. "You lay another finger on them—Sierra, Shana, or anyone associated with them—and it won't just be personal. It'll be your funeral."

The threat hangs in the air, heavy and unmistakable. I hear his sharp intake of breath, the first crack in his cocky façade. He knows exactly who I am and, more importantly, what I can do.

I've seen the fear in men's eyes when they realize their time is up. Jackson's would be no different.

"All right, all right," he mutters, the bravado slipping from his tone. "No need to get dramatic, man. Just get me the cash, and we'll call it even."

"Even?" I bite back, my voice sharp enough to cut through steel. "You think this is about money? This isn't a transaction, Jackson. This is a lesson. You don't touch what's mine, and you don't mess with my family."

He's quiet for a beat too long, and I know the wheels are turning in his head. He remembers Jason—the man who thought he could snatch his sister, my fiancée, Vee, away from me without consequences. Jason's still walking, but he's a shadow of the man he used to be. Jackson saw the aftermath, and he knows exactly how far I'll go to protect what's mine. His brother-in-law's lifetime limp is a testament to that. Everyone in Chesapeake Heights knows I only left one breath in that fool's body.

"I hear you," Jackson says finally, his voice laced with a thin veneer of bravado. "But let's not forget, Freeman, you're not squeaky clean yourself. A man like you... you've got skeletons. Just sayin'."

I smirk, cold and calculating. "Oh, I've got skeletons, that's for sure. But here's the thing, Jackson—I also have leverage.

Let's not forget what my day job involves. If I can counter international terrorists, I can certainly unravel your piecemeal organization. After all, information is power."

His silence tells me he knows exactly what I'm talking about. The background check I ran on him through the dark web turned up everything—his offshore accounts, illegal businesses, even surveillance footage that ties him to things he thought he'd covered up. I've got enough to bury him under the kind of federal charges that make even the boldest criminals sweat.

"You've got two choices, Jackson," I say, my voice steady and unforgiving. "Stay away from Sierra and keep breathing, or keep playing with me and lose everything. Tick-tock."

He swallows audibly, the sound loud enough to echo through the phone. "Fine," he spits. "But I want my money tonight."

Bitchass.

I hang up on him but don't move, my mind racing. This isn't over—not by a long shot. Jackson might think he's calling the shots, but he doesn't realize he's already lost. I've got the upper hand, and when I'm done, he won't just regret touching Sierra and her family—he'll regret ever saying her name.

I exhale, the weight of my promise settling on my shoulders. I text an associate of mine to make the drop-off to Jackson tonight. This isn't about money. I'd pay ten times as much if I had to. It's about Sierra. About making sure she never has to face fear again.

"Sierra Watson is mine," I say into the empty room, my voice low but sure. The air here carries my vow, salt-tinged and solemn. I'm not some ghost of false promises like Vee. I'm here. I'm real. And I'll stand between her and any storm life throws her way.

A small, dark smile tugs at my lips. Because deep down, I

know this grumpy soul of mine thrives on being her sunshine. And I'll burn bright enough to chase away every shadow chasing her.

I'm about to text Amara an update when the sliding doors whoosh open like some damn dramatic entrance in a soap opera. Except this isn't fiction, and it isn't glamorous.

Sierra rushes in, her wild auburn curls a tangled testament to her panic. Shana limps beside her, clutching her side. Nurses swarm them, efficient as ants at a picnic, whisking Shana away. Sierra's eyes—those deep wells of desperation—lock on to mine. She crumbles like a building gutted by fire, and all strength turns to ash.

"Jabari!" The cry rips from her throat, raw and ragged.

I catch her before she hits the ground, her body trembling against mine. "Easy, baby," I murmur, wrapping her up in arms that have known more war than warmth. "You're safe now. You're with me." Words aren't my strong suit, but for her, I'll spin a damn soliloquy if it keeps the terror from her eyes.

She clings to me, her sobs racking through her like a hurricane through the bay, and I hold on tighter, wondering if she feels the tremors running under my skin—the aftershocks of a heart that's learned to beat for someone else.

"Jabari?!"

My sister, Amara, strides into the waiting room, elegance personified, even in crisis mode. She stops short at the sight of us, and I can almost hear the cogs turning in her head, recalibrating every image she's had of her big brother—the grump who'd sooner face a storm head-on than deal with a tearful woman.

"Sierra?" Amara's voice is a soothing balm, and her presence is the gentle touch I called her for. She kneels beside us, reaching out to stroke Sierra's arm. "It's going to be okay, sweetheart."

Sierra's cries soften, her breath hitching as she lifts her head to look at Amara. There's a flicker of relief in her gaze, and she nods, still gasping for air like each breath is a lifeboat in these treacherous waters.

"Thank you for coming," I say, my voice gravelly with unspoken gratitude. Amara always had a way of making sense of my storms, of smoothing the edges of my too-sharp concern.

"Always," Amara replies, a smile touching her lips as she watches Sierra, now quiet, curled in my lap. Her expression shifts—surprise, joy, maybe a dash of disbelief—as she takes in the scene. "I've never seen you so... tender."

"Mark it on your calendar," I grunt, the corner of my mouth lifting despite myself. "It might just be a once-in-a-lifetime event."

"Or the start of something new," Amara counters, her eyes twinkling with that knowing look that says she's already picturing Sierra at Sunday dinners, part of the fold.

"Maybe," I concede, feeling the protective walls around my heart crack a bit more. Because here, with Sierra shivering in my embrace and Amara ready to back me up, I'm reminded of what's worth fighting for—family, love, and a woman who's shown me the light without trying.

"Let's get through tonight first," I add, because hope is dangerous, and I've had enough surprises to last a lifetime. But as Sierra's breath evens out against my chest, I let myself believe, if only for a moment, that in this small-town romance we're writing, the beast gets his beauty after all.

* * *

Sierra wakes up from her catnap an hour later, groggy and asking for her sister. She was so exhausted when she got here that she fell asleep in my embrace. I won't lie and say it didn't feel like she belonged in my arms, because it did. Now, I don't want her ever to leave my embrace.

"Hey," Amara says, waving a small card before a still-dazed

Sierra. She blinks and refocuses on the piece of paper. "My number," Amara smiles and whispers. Don't make me chase you for a lunch date next week. I'm here if you need to talk. We're all too familiar with the Taylors and their antics."

With eyes that hold more worry than the storm clouds outside, Sierra manages a weak smile and takes the card. "I won't," she murmurs, her voice a fragile thread in the thick tension of the clinic. "Thank you for coming."

She stands to hug Amara, and I begrudgingly let her go.

"Of course. You're family now." Amara's firm embrace of Sierra is a testament to our upbringing—Freemans take care of their own. She moves in, wrapping Sierra in a hug that's both a shield and a salve. Then it's my turn, and I'm engulfed in an embrace that smells like home and stubborn hope. "Take care of her, Jabari," she whispers into my ear, her breath warm against the chill nipping at my resolve.

"Always," I reply, my grip on Sierra tightening by a fraction. Amara pulls away, her eyes searching mine for a trace of the brother who once believed love was a battlefield where no one was left unscarred. Whatever she sees softens her gaze before she turns and strides out of the medical center, leaving us in a bubble of uncertainty that pops the moment the doctor appears.

"Ms. Watson," he begins, his voice steady, "your sister sustained two broken ribs, a sprained ankle, a broken arm, and a concussion."

"Is she—" Sierra starts, but the doc raises a hand to halt her spiral into panic.

"She's been sedated for now. She won't be up for talking until tomorrow. You should see her for a moment, then go home. Rest. Come back in the morning."

The word 'home' hits a nerve, and Sierra shakes her head,

her curls bouncing with the vehemence of her refusal. She leaves my lap and stands. "I'm not leaving her."

"Ms. Watson..." The doctor's patience is saintly, but mine is wearing thin. I stand, tugging gently on her arm. "Come on, baby. Your sister's in good hands. Let's head back to Baycrest and let her body heal. You can stay with me tonight."

"My place is here," she fires back, defiance lacing her tone. I recognize the stubborn set to her jaw, the way she's ready to dig her heels in and fight the world if she must. This drew me to her —this fiery spirit wrapped in a softness that could calm the fiercest storms—including the ones raging inside me.

"Listen," I say, my voice low and even, "Shana's safe here. But you're barely holding yourself together. You need rest. And I... I need to know you're safe, too. Please, stay with me tonight."

She hesitates, caught between the urge to battle on and the pull of something new—us. Her eyes meet mine, and I see the flicker of trust, bright and daring.

"Okay," she finally whispers, her surrender wrapped in the strength to let someone else share the load.

"Good." A wry smile touches my lips as I scoop her up, cradling her close while we navigate the maze of sterile hallways to Shana's room. "Because I wasn't about to let you win this one."

"Of course not," Sierra replies, her laugh brittle but real. "Can't let the beast lose face."

"Damn right," I chuckle, feeling the weight of the world shift just enough to let a sliver of light through the cracks.

EIGHTEEN

Joy and Pain

SIERRA

As I cross the threshold of Baycrest, the familiar scent of salty bay air mixed with a hint of ancient oak becomes more than just an occupational aroma. This time, it feels different—it's not my crisp polo and the director's badge that bring me here, but the prospect of spending the night wrapped in something other than loneliness. Jabari's presence behind me offers towering assurance, his hand gently pressing on the small of my back, guiding me forward.

"Come on upstairs, baby," he murmurs, his voice a soft command that sends a shiver down my spine.

"Baby" again, that term of endearment that should feel cliché but instead has me coming undone at the knees. Who knew two syllables could pack such a punch? The tingling sensation of nervous excitement snakes through me, a cocktail of fear and desire that makes me want to bolt and surrender all at once.

We ascend the grand staircase, every step an escalation of the night's promises. My heart thumps in a frantic rhythm like it's trying to break free and run ahead of us. But Jabari's steady and unwavering touch keeps me grounded, even as my thoughts spiral.

He opens the door to a guest room that's straight from some luxury fantasy. Whites, golds, and creams blend in a symphony of elegance that steals my breath. I gasp, taking it all in. The room feels like a tangible whisper of wealth and comfort, a sanctuary designed for the likes of which I'm not sure I belong.

"You'll sleep here tonight," Jabari announces, and there's a note of something tender in his voice that I don't want to examine too closely for fear it might just be my imagination.

"Will you—uh—stay with me?" The words tumble out before I can stop them, a reluctant plea from a place inside me that doesn't want to admit how much I dread being alone in this vast sea of opulence.

"Until I fall asleep?"

It's not just the room that's intimidating—it's everything— the stormy beginning, the unexpected rescue, the way my body seems to recognize him as its true north. And now, this room, so beautiful it almost hurts, is a stark reminder of the distance between the world I know and the one Jabari inhabits.

"Of course, Sierra." A smile in his voice matches the curve of those full lips I've been aching to taste again. "I'm not going anywhere."

He pulls me into his arms, and I let out a silent breath of relief, feeling a little more anchored in the hurricane of emotions that Jabari stirs within me. Maybe I'm playing with fire. Perhaps I'm walking into the eye of the storm, but if

Jabari's at the center of it, it's exactly where I'm supposed to be.

"You'll never be alone again," Jabari murmurs against my lips before his mouth descends on mine with a passion that steals my breath and all coherent thought. It's the kind of kiss that seizes control, assertive and deep, igniting flames in places I forgot could burn. His hands cradle my face, and I'm lost to the taste of him—dark coffee mixed with something innately masculine that belongs to him alone.

At this moment, claimed is not just a word; it's a raw, thrilling sensation that spreads through every fiber of my being. It's a declaration made without a single spoken promise, branded by the press of his lips against mine. Since Mama left this earth untethered, I've yearned for an anchor, someone to belong to who would hold fast against life's relentless tides. And damn it, if Jabari's kiss doesn't feel like coming home—like I'm his.

"Baby, you need to eat." His voice breaks through the haze of desire, and I almost protest until I see the sincere concern etched in the lines of his face. "Let me take care of you."

I want to scoff at needing anyone to look after me. I'm self-sufficient to a fault. But there's no denying the tremor in my limbs or the way my stomach tightens, not from hunger but from a nervous energy that has nothing to do with food. "I'm not hungry," I manage to say, but the words sound feeble even to my ears.

"Non-negotiable." The command rolls off his tongue wrapped in velvet, yet as unyielding as steel. This man, who bears the weight of family legacy on shoulders broad enough to carry it, won't be swayed. And I find, to my surprise, that his high-handedness isn't chafing as it should. Instead, it wraps around my fluttering heart like a protective glove. Somehow, his insistence feels like care, not control.

"I'm going to draw a bath for you," he says, already plotting a course of action while my mind still swims in the aftermath of his kiss. "You'll wait for me in the tub when I'm done; I'll bring up something to eat."

"Okay," I breathe out, the word less of an agreement and more a surrender to the current pulling me under. There's no use fighting the tide when every cell in your body wants to be swept away.

I follow him into the bathroom and lean against the cool marble doorframe, watching Jabari's hands, sure and steady from years of military precision, twist the vintage brass taps. The rush of water fills the white clawfoot tub, starkly contrasting the warm golds and creams that decorate the room. It's like stepping into a page from one of those interior design magazines I thumb through but never buy.

"Like what you see?" His voice is a low purr, his hazel eyes catching mine in the mirror as he bends over and swirls lavender oil into the water.

"Very much," I confess without a shred of shame, my gaze lingering on the firmness of his backside before skittering away. He answers my drooling with a quick wink and a knowing smirk. It should embarrass me, being caught ogling him like some lovesick teenager, but it doesn't. It feels like this whole night is a series of puzzle pieces clicking into place.

He stands and passes me in the doorway before heading downstairs to get our food. "Be good, Sierra." He brushes a peck on my cheek, leaving a trail of warmth that conflicts with the shiver down my spine. "I'll be back soon."

"Define 'good,'" I tease, but he's already gone. The echo of his laughter is a soft promise in the vast bathroom.

The tub is an oasis, and I waste no time shedding my clothes, letting them fall in a heap on the plush rug. The lavender scent rises with the steam, curling around me like a lover's caress. As I lower myself into the water, the heat seeps into my bones, unknotting the tension I've held for too long.

Minutes or hours could have passed when the door opens again, but who's counting? Not me; I'm lost in the haze of warm water and warmer thoughts.

"Hope you're hungry." Jabari's figure looms over me, a charcuterie tray in one hand and a bottle of red in the other—his personal brand of artillery.

"Starving," I lie, because it's easier than admitting that the emptiness in my stomach has nothing to do with food.

He feeds me olives and cheeses, fingers brushing my lips, each touch igniting sparks traveling south. The wine is robust, a perfect complement to the man who pours it. We don't talk much; words are superfluous when our bodies are having their own conversation.

"Let me," he says, setting the tray aside, and there's a command in his tone that I don't want to defy.

His hands move over my body, washing away more than just stress and the physical day. They sweep along curves and press into muscles, a choreography mapped out by instinct. When his fingers skim close to where I'm most vulnerable, it's all I can do not to arch into his touch like a flower seeking sunlight.

"I shouldn't enjoy your bossiness this much," I murmur, my voice coming out breathier than intended.

"Yet, here we are," he replies, a hint of dark humor lacing his words.

By the time he's done, I'm something molten, shaped by his hands, ready to solidify at his command. My heart hammers a frenetic rhythm, a silent plea for more, for everything.

"Need anything else, Sierra?" he asks, and oh, how his tone skirts the edge of propriety.

"Everything," I admit, because what's the point of

pretending when every nerve ending screams his name? "Everything you're willing to give."

His arms are a cradle of command as Jabari lifts me from the bath, water trailing down my skin like the afterthoughts of his touch. Wrapped in the plush towel he provides, I am carried through to the bedroom—a realm now stripped of any pretense. The air is dense with anticipation, which thickens your blood and sharpens your senses.

He places me on my feet beside the bed, the towel falls away, and his eyes roam over me—intense, assessing, predatory. My heart thunders against my ribs, echoing the hunger I see mirrored in him.

"Turn around," he orders, voice low and tinged with a darkness that thrills me. I obey, feeling his gaze like a physical caress along the curve of my back.

"Jabari," I plead without shame, "touch me again."

He doesn't respond with words. Instead, he stalks around me, a grin pulling at the edges of his mouth, but his eyes never lose focus. I am his prey, willingly caught in the snare of his attention.

He strides toward me, muscles rippling under his shirt as he effortlessly lifts and tosses me onto the plush bed. His gaze sweeps over my body, filled with hunger and desire.

"Show me what's mine," he growls, his commanding tone sending a shiver of excitement through me. In one swift motion, I spread my legs wide and offer myself to him.

With power and skill, he devours me with his mouth, igniting a fire deep within that spreads through every inch of my being. He licks the outside of my core like an ice cream cone he's searched for and finally found before nibbling on my clit like the savage beast he is. The sounds of him slurping my juices while moaning in pleasure make me gush all over his face. When

I look down, he's opening his mouth to drink at my fountain, and I'm gone.

My fingers clutch at the sheets as pleasure cascades over me in waves, his name a desperate plea on my lips.

The room spins, my body trembles, and I am consumed by an inferno of pleasure that only grows more intense as he continues to claim me relentlessly. At this moment, I am nothing but sparks and flames, burning brightly under his touch until I am reduced to ashes in the aftermath.

"Damn, Jabari," I breathe out once I can form thoughts again. His chuckle is deep, vibrating against my sensitized flesh, and I know this is just the beginning. With his unwavering control and care, this man has unraveled me—and I've never been more willing to be undone.

NINETEEN

Sharing the Night Together

I STAND, WIPING SIERRA'S JUICES FROM MY MOUTH and beard. She tastes like heaven, and I know I'm already addicted.

She keeps her eyes on me as my clothes hit the floor, fabric whispering promises of what's to come.

Sierra—damn, she's a vision all laid out on my bed, skin glowing under the dim light like she's been kissed by Oshun herself. Tremors rack her body, little aftershocks from the pleasure I've already given her, and it's a sight that could bring a man to his knees—if I weren't already standing tall.

"Nothing," I growl, voice rough as gravel, "nothing gets me harder than watching you come apart for me." The condom slides over me, tight and secure, a promise of what's to follow. Inside, my heart's a damn drum line; the anticipation of fully being with her is electric, buzzing through my veins. I've fantasized about being inside her, to feel her wrapped around me, and it's got me vibrating with need.

"Jabari... please." Sierra's soft, pleading voice pulls me down like gravity. As I cover her body with mine, I can't help but think how right it feels—the weight of my body pressing down on her, the fit of us together. I capture her mouth with mine, a kiss so hot it could start fires, and for a moment, we're lost in it, tongues tangling, breath mingling.

Pulling back, I lock eyes with her. "What do you need, Sierra, baby? All you have to do is ask." The game's afoot, and I'm not about to let her off easy—not when I know she's close, teetering on the edge of something monumental.

I pull back just enough to lock eyes with her, my voice dropping low. "Just say the word baby, and I'll give it to you." The tension crackles between us, thick and hot, and I can see it—her submission to this moment is right there.

"Jabari..." She moans, and the sound goes straight to my dick. Her hips rotate, seeking, pushing her pussy closer to where we both want it to be.

"Tell me," I press, my voice low and rough as I hover over her, close enough to catch the intoxicating scent of her arousal. The air between us hums, thick with expectation and something darker—something that pulls us both in, like the tide dragging us under.

It's a game, a dance, where I lead and she follows. But only if she's ready. Only if she's brave enough to say it out loud.

There's power in asking for what you want. And Sierra—my stunning, stubborn Siren—is about to discover just how much power she truly has.

She bucks her hips up against mine with a moan that almost makes me break my resolve. "Unh, unh, beautiful," I chuckle darkly, the sound rumbling from deep within my chest. Sierra's wide eyes, glazed with desire, meet mine, and I know she's close to begging. I want her words; they're as necessary as breath. "You've got to tell me what you want. I need to hear the words." My voice is a low command tempered with a playfulness that only we understand. "What do you need, Sierra, baby?"

Her body writhes beneath me, a beautiful testament to the urgency of her need. And then, finally, it spills forth—a desperate scream filled with raw honesty and vulnerability: "You! I need you, Jabari!"

With a fierce determination, I plunge into her, feeling the resistance and yielding of her body with each inch.

"Fuck, Sierra, baby. You feel so good squeezing my dick like that," I whisper in her ear as our passion ignites like wildfire.

We're consumed as we build to an explosive crescendo. Time stands still as I conduct a symphony of bliss inside her walls, every stroke and movement in perfect harmony, each second a powerful note that echoes through our bodies.

"God, yes," she groans as her tight warmth envelops me. This pleasure is a living thing, coursing through our veins with every push deeper into her. At her ear, my words flow like honey, sweet and thick with lust. "You're such a good girl, Sierra. Made for me."

My hips speed up in a primal dance, driven by a fierce urgency to claim her. Each thrust maps out the contours of our connection, tracing the contours of our desire. Her thick thighs are soft and yielding in my grasp as I lever them back, baring her entirely to my gaze, to my hunger. This is more than just sex; it feels like worship. It is an all-consuming ritual that marks us irreversibly, merging our souls into one.

"Jabari!" Her cries rip from her throat, a melody that stirs the protective beast within me. I pound into her, relentless, each drive a promise etched in pleasure. My world narrows to the slick heat of her, the way her body grips me, the sounds of our union filling the room.

"More, Sierra, give me more," I demand between gritted teeth, an instinctual part of me taking over. This dance is ours alone, and I'm leading us both to the brink and beyond. She's my sunshine in the storm, my unexpected salvation, and I'll be damned if I don't reverence her with every fiber of my being.

I'm lost in the beat, the heat, the pure, unadulterated bond that binds me to Sierra. Every thrust is a revelation, every gasp from her lips a testament to what we've found here, skin to skin, soul to soul. I've been a fool, letting shadows of betrayal cage my heart when, all along, it yearned for this—for her.

"Sierra," I growl, burying myself deeper, "nothing has ever felt this right." The words are half prayer, half vow as they escape me, an oath etched in the sweat and fervor of our joining. She's my balm, my redemption—the one who turns the page on a story marred by past hurts.

Her screams crescendo, a cacophony of pleasure that echoes through the chambers of my heart. And as she shatters under me, convulsing in ecstasy, I'm already plotting her next ascent. "Again," I demand, my voice a husky command, "come for me again, Sierra, baby."

She shakes her head, breathless, spent. But I know her strength, her boundless capacity for joy. Leaning down, I gently cup her throat, feeling the thrum of her pulse against my palm. My mouth finds her cheek, nipping softly. "You can come for me again, can't you, baby?" I tilt her hips up to get a deeper angle. "You can do anything... Ready?"

It's not just a question—it's a promise. My hand descends, fingers finding her, playing her body like an instrument tuned just for me as I plunge deeper and deeper into sweet pussy. The wet sounds of our joining fill the room as she erupts beneath my touch, a beautiful explosion of sensation that sends her soaring once more.

As she crests that wave, I let out a fierce roar as I ride the wave of pleasure, shattering any barriers between us. I remove the condom, and my release shoots out, coating her stomach like a brand, marking her as mine in a wild display of passion and possession. At that moment, I swear to myself that my seed will be planted deep inside her next time, claiming her entirely as my own.

There's a rawness, a keen satisfaction in watching my essence paint her skin. It's a canvas I intend to revisit, each brushstroke a declaration of love, of permanence. I run my fingers through my seed and feed her a taste from my fingers. She eagerly licks me dry and moans.

"Fuck..." I groan as I take her mouth in another searing kiss until we're both breathless. She's my Siren, an unexpected ally in a world bent on testing my resolve. She's mine, now and always.

Gasping for air, my lungs greedy for every ounce of oxygen, I collapse beside Sierra, the bed still echoing our passion. A quiver runs through me, a tremor of pure, unadulterated pleasure, and I can't help but pull her atop me, needing to feel her weight, grounding me to reality.

"Sierra," I murmur, my voice rougher than the gravel roads leading into Chesapeake Heights. My hands roam her back, tracing the arches and valleys of her spine. "You good?"

"More than okay," she breathes out, her voice a soothing and unnerving melody in its vulnerability. I feel tears fall to my chest, and I'm immediately on high alert. Damn it, did I push too hard?

Rolling her onto her back, I prop myself on an elbow, looming over her like a concerned guardian. "Talk to me, Sierra baby. What's got you crying?" I ask, brushing a tear away with the pad of my thumb, feeling like I'm tiptoeing around landmines.

Her eyes, wide and shimmering, lock on to mine. "Jabari,

I've never... what we just did... it's overwhelming." She pauses, catching her breath, her chest rising and falling under my gaze. "But in the best way."

I let out a breath I didn't realize I was holding, relief washing over me like the bay's tides. Smiling, I lean down and capture her lips in a kiss meant to seal promises and chase away fears. It's deep and thorough, a testament to new beginnings and unspoken oaths. I want to tell her I've fallen in love, but I know my girl may not be ready. Hell, it just became clear to me tonight when she called me in tears, and I was prepared to tear the world apart for her. So, instead, I tell her the next best thing.

"Listen to me, Sierra," I say, pulling back just enough to speak, my forehead resting against hers. "You'll never have to worry about a damn thing again. You hear me? I've got you. Always."

She nods, her tears subsiding, as if my words are the balm to soothe all her past hurts. And hell, I mean every word. The Freeman family might be known for its strength and endurance, but this woman beneath me—she's my foundation now.

With the stress of the evening fading to a distant memory, we succumb to exhaustion, our bodies entwined, finding solace in the shared warmth. As sleep claims us, I make a silent promise to her and myself. I'll be her shelter, her sanctuary in every tempest life throws our way. Because Sierra Watson is more than my soulmate—she's the missing piece I never knew I needed until she washed ashore, turning my world upside down.

And with that thought cradling my mind, I let the darkness take me, knowing that when dawn breaks over Chesapeake Heights, it'll shine on a new chapter for us—one where fear has no place and love reigns supreme.

TWENTY

Fortress Around Your Heart

THE SUN BLAZES HIGH IN THE SKY, POURING through the windows and daring me to keep my eyes closed any longer. With a half-asleep blink, I surrender and glance at the digital clock on the nightstand. Ten a.m. Ten. It's a personal best for someone like me who rarely lets the world spin this far without diving in.

A slow smile tugs at my lips as flashes of last night sweep through my mind. Jabari's hands, his lips, the way he claimed me without hesitation—completely and utterly. Damn, the man knows how to leave a mark.

I shift in the softest sheets ever and reach instinctively for the warm body that should still be tangled in these sheets with me, but all I find is cool linen. My chest tightens, the disappointment brief but sharp.

Then I spot it—a neatly folded note resting on his pillow.

My heart skips a beat as I pluck it up, his clean, deliberate script catching my eye. *Good morning, Siren. Come downstairs whenever you're ready. I've got breakfast and coffee for you.*

Siren. That nickname never fails to pull a blush to my cheeks. It's his way of reminding me that he sees me as something magnetic, something impossible to resist. But even his sweet words can't keep the shadows at bay. My mind wanders, unbidden, to Shana.

"She needs to handle her own mess, Sierra," I mutter, swinging my legs off the bed and letting the mantra echo through the room. It's a lie, of course. Shana's mess *is* my mess. It always has been. Her gambling feels like a lit match on dry kindling, threatening to spark a wildfire through my reputation. If word of it spreads through Chesapeake Heights—my idyllic little haven—it won't just be idle gossip over mimosas. It'll be a scandal, the kind that sticks.

The Freemans don't need more drama. They've already had their fair share, thank you very much. But Shana? She's my sister. And even when she screws up—and boy, does she screw up—I protect her. I *fix* things. It's what I do. My independence didn't come easily, and I won't let anyone take it from me—not Shana's mistakes, not the whispers of nosy resort guests, and not my self-doubt.

I let out a long breath, squaring my shoulders. Jabari's note is too sweet for the storm brewing in my mind. But the man means well, and right now, I'll take the coffee and whatever strength his presence offers. Still, I know better than to lean on anyone for long.

I pad across the room, my resolve hardening with each step. Whatever comes next, I'll handle it. I always do. Siren or not, I know this isn't the kind of fairy tale where a knight rides in to save the day.

The door creaks open, and there he is—Jabari, all six-feet-five inches of commanding presence filling the room. His frame cuts a silhouette against the hallway light, a plate balanced in one hand like it belongs there—his brow furrows, severe and focused, as his eyes find mine. Without hesitation, he strides in, closes the door with his foot, and bends down to press a kiss against my lips. It's warm, slow, and deep, sweeping away the last remnants of sleep like a tide reclaiming the shore.

"Changed my mind, Siren," he says, his voice a smooth current, warm and thick like molasses. "Breakfast in bed today."

The rich aroma of pecan waffles wafts between us, and I can't help but be impressed. It's the kind of decadence Jabari creates effortlessly—like the caramel-infused whipped cream I spot on the plate. He knows me too well; he knows I'll take a bite before I push back. And he's right. One bite in, and I'm momentarily undone by the buttery sweetness, the salty crunch of bacon. It's indulgent, over the top, and entirely Jabari.

But I'm not in the mood to indulge for long. I set the fork down and draw a steadying breath, already feeling the day's weight pressing in. "This is sweet, really, but I need to get going to meet Shana at the hospital and—"

"Sierra." His voice cuts through my excuses like a blade—firm, unyielding, but threaded with care. He steps closer, his hazel eyes locking on to mine, his hand brushing a stray curl from my face. "You're running on fumes, baby girl. Shana can wait. You need to eat first."

His logic makes sense, but I hate that it does. I hate how he reads me so well and how his determination chips away at mine. I hate how he can call me baby girl, and my entire body lights up in submission. Still, I let him guide another bite of waffle to my lips, savoring the sweetness against my better judgment. But before I can fully lose myself in the moment, he drops a bomb —words I never saw coming but absolutely should have.

"I paid off Shana's debts."

The words hit me like a lightning strike, igniting every nerve. My body tenses, my heart pounding like a war drum. "Paid off her debts?" The words spill from my lips, sharp and incredulous. I sit up, the spell of breakfast broken. "What makes you think I needed you to clean up my sister's mess?"

He doesn't flinch. He never does. His expression remains steady, a storm brewing just beneath the surface. "Sierra, I just wanted to help."

"Help?" My voice rises, taking on an edge as I swing my legs over the side of the bed. "Or control? Because there's a difference, Jabari, and you're dangerously close to crossing it. Did you even think to ask me what I wanted?"

His jaw tightens, and I can see the frustration flare in his hazel eyes. "You're twisting this into something it's not. I can't stand by and watch you shoulder this alone when I can make it disappear."

"Make it disappear?" My laugh is brittle, my hands curling into fists at my sides. "You think throwing money at Shana's problems will fix everything? That's not how this works. That's not how *I* work."

He rakes a hand over his close-cropped hair, his frustration simmering. "Why do you have to be so damn stubborn?"

"Because it's my life!" The words burst out of me, raw and unfiltered. I stand, pacing the room, my curls wild around my face as I spin to face him again. "I get to decide how to handle my family's problems. Not you. Not anyone else. Me."

Jabari takes a step closer, his voice softer now but steady, the kind of calm that carries weight. "This isn't about control, Sierra. It's about trust. Trusting that I want what's best for you."

His words hang between us, but before I can respond, he pushes forward, his hazel eyes locking onto mine. "I didn't tell you before because I didn't want to embarrass you. But I overheard you on the beach that day. I heard you talking about Dominion, and I knew there was probably a mess with Jackson Taylor."

The mention of Jackson's name hits like a punch to the gut, the breath rushing from me. I freeze, my arms falling limp at my sides. He knows everything, and he didn't even say anything. Not at dinner, not when we were walking by the bay, not even after he was balls-deep inside of me. *He must think I'm pathetic.*

I'm about a second from raging in this room or having a panic attack from shame, and he doesn't even notice. He keeps going.

"Jackson is my ex-fiancé's brother, Sierra," he continues, his voice lowering, a sharp edge cutting through his calm. "I know what kind of demon he turns into when money is involved. I've seen it firsthand. When you brought your sister into the infirmary last night, I knew it wasn't just her health that needed fixing. He wouldn't stop, Sierra. Not unless someone stepped in."

He pauses, letting the words settle like stones in the quiet air. "So, I called him. Wired him the money. And I told him if he so much as *looks* your way—or Shana's—I'll kill him. And I meant every word."

The room tilts, his confession colliding with every raw nerve inside me. My pulse thrums in my ears, drowning out the sound of my breath. Jabari stands there, solid and unyielding, his hands clenched at his sides, his body coiled like he's ready to act on his promise at any moment.

"You *what?*" My voice cracks, disbelief and anger warring for control. My mind scrambles to catch up, to process the enormity of what he's just said. He didn't just cross a line—he bulldozed over it.

"I did what I had to do," he says, his tone unflinching, his eyes boring into mine. "Because I wasn't going to sit back and watch him ruin your lives. Not Shana's, not yours. You're too important to me."

My stomach twists; the words that should sound like protection instead of ringing with suffocation. "Jabari, you had no right—"

"I had *every* right," he interrupts, his voice firm but not raised. "Because you were drowning, Sierra. I saw it, even if you didn't want me to. I didn't ask for permission because I wasn't about to let your pride or stubbornness get in the way of keeping you safe."

I shake my head, taking a step back, needing the distance, needing air. "You think this fixes everything? You think paying him off and making threats will make this disappear?"

"It's a start," he replies, his gaze unwavering. "And it's more than anyone else has done for you."

The words hit their mark, cutting deep, but instead of softening me, they ignited a fire. "You don't get to decide that!" I snap, my voice rising as I throw up my hands. "You don't get to come in, take over, and act like you know what's best for me!"

Jabari doesn't flinch, his expression resolute. "I didn't act out of control, Sierra. I acted out of love. There's a difference."

The word—*love*—lingers in the space between us, but it doesn't feel like a balm. It feels like a sharp and intrusive blade cutting through the fragile balance of what we had. And for the first time, I wonder if Jabari's love is too much. Too heavy. Too consuming.

Because right now, it feels like I'm drowning.

"Trust?" I cross my arms, the armor I know too well. "You swooping in without saying a word to me—without telling me you knew the man who's been tormenting me—feels like you're telling me you don't trust *me* to handle it. Like I can't handle my life."

"That's not fair," he says quietly, his voice almost breaking.

"First, this isn't your life; it's your sister's. It's her problem, not yours. I know you love her, but you can't throw away your life to save hers. I won't allow it."

His words feel like a slap, but I don't respond, and he keeps talking.

"Second, I trust you more than anyone."

"Then act like it." I turn away from him, staring at the calm, unbothered Chesapeake Bay through a window. The waves lap at the shore, indifferent to the storm raging inside me. "Because this? This doesn't feel like trust. It feels like domination."

He doesn't say anything, but I can feel him behind me, the weight of his presence thick and heavy. Finally, he reaches out, his hand brushing my shoulder.

"Enough," I say, my voice barely above a whisper, but the word carries the weight of everything unsaid. "I need space, Jabari. I can't do this right now."

His hand falls away, the distance between us growing in ways I can't measure.

"Space," he repeats, the word more question than confirmation.

"Space," I say again, my voice firmer this time; even as my heart fractures into pieces, I don't know if I can put it back together.

"No." He growls, "You need love, not—"

A reverberating crash downstairs cuts through our heated exchange like a thunderclap, silencing the room and jolting my pulse into overdrive. I hear my sister scream my name from downstairs, and Jabari's voice fades into the background as my instincts kick in, overriding every thought but one: *Shana.*

Why isn't she in the hospital?

I tear out of the bedroom, my bare feet skimming the polished wood floors as I bolt down the grand staircase. Behind me, I hear Jabari's sharp protests, but they are swallowed by the chaotic clamor echoing through Baycrest's opulent halls.

"Shana!" I call her name, the sound trembling on the edge of panic. My heart pounds as I descend into a scene that can only be described as a public disaster. The foyer has become a battle-field, spectators forming a tight ring around the epicenter of chaos—my sister.

TWENTY-ONE

Emotion

SIERRA

LORD, HELP!

Shana is standing in the foyer of Baycrest, wild-eyed and defiant, her hospital gown barely hidden beneath a hastily thrown-on cardigan. She's screaming at the poor concierge, who's trying to calm her down. "You've got no right to talk to me like that!" She shouts, her voice cutting through the murmur of onlookers like jagged glass. "I'm *fine*!"

Fine? Fine is a hospital bed and an IV drip, not this—this breakdown in the middle of the resort's reception area. My stomach twists as I push through the crowd, every instinct screaming to shield her from the sea of judgmental stares. This isn't just a scene; it's the unraveling of everything I've tried so damn hard to protect.

I reach my sister in seconds and pull her to the side, careful not to hurt her injuries. "What are you doing here? You're supposed to be in the hospital," I harshly whisper.

She snatches her arm from my grasp, and I notice the wince. "I broke out of there before somebody killed me. I told you, no hospitals! What? Do you want Jackson to come and kill me? That's just like you, Sierra. Throw me away as soon as I become too much to handle. You've probably been waiting for a way to get rid of me. Just like I should have gotten rid of you when mom died and let you suffer in the system." She lifts her hand to strike me, but I catch it mid-air.

"You ungrateful bitch!" She screams at me, and my heart breaks.

I look at her in shock and barely notice that Jabari is at my side. The room is so quiet; everyone's eyes are on me and my mess. I choke back a sob and drop Shana's arm. She looks at me like I'm the devil, and I almost double over in emotional pain.

"Sierra," Amara's calm voice slices through the rising panic buzzing in my ears. Her hand finds my arm, anchoring me in place. "Let me handle this. Go with Jabari."

I freeze, torn between charging ahead and trusting Jabari's steady presence. *I just told him I needed space.*

Amara steps past me, radiating an effortless authority that pauses the tension in the room. She turns to the crowd, her voice like silk but with an edge that commands obedience.

"Ladies and gentlemen, please return to your activities," she says, her tone smooth and unyielding. "There's nothing to worry about here. We appreciate your understanding."

Some of the whispers die, and the knot of spectators begins to dissolve, their curiosity somewhat pacified. However, a few are at the front desk demanding to know what kind of place allows something like this to happen. I hear one lady ask the concierge if she's safe.

I stand rooted in place, watching with awe and frustration

as Amara, in seconds, does what I've been struggling to do for years: contain Shana's chaos.

Amara turns to my sister, her tone softening but still firm. "Shana, you're scaring the guests and your sister," she says, stepping closer, her movements deliberate and calm. "Let's talk about this somewhere private, okay?"

Shana's shoulders slump, her defiance draining away like air from a punctured balloon. She suddenly looks so tiny and fragile against the room's grandeur, breaking my heart. Amara wraps an arm around her waist, leading her away with a patience I could never seem to muster regarding Shana.

Behind me, I feel the heat of Jabari's hand on my back, grounding me in a way I didn't realize I needed. I'm unsure whether it's a silent offer of support or his way of bridging the gap left by our earlier argument. But his touch reminds me of a truth I've been trying to ignore: I need him.

I glance toward Amara, watching her disappear with Shana down a corridor. My voice is barely a whisper. "Thank you," I murmur, though what I mean is, *how do I fix this?*

Jabari's hand tightens gently around mine, but even his strength can't erase the sinking feeling in my chest. I release from his hold, not knowing if I'm drowning in my sister's chaos or my own, but either way, the added pressure of being good enough for him makes the weight unbearable.

The front doors burst open, and Asa strides into the room like a gust of fresh air. Amara must have called him. His presence instantly shifts the atmosphere, and his calm confidence radiates from every step. Heads turn, and the murmurs quiet as his polished shoes glide over the marble floor. He maneuvers through overturned chairs and Shana's wreckage with the ease of someone who thrives in chaos.

"All right now, folks," he says, his voice smooth and rich, like the saxophone solos playing late at night in the resort lounge. "Let's not let a little excitement ruin the mood. How about we trade those frowns for some signature Chesapeake Heights smiles, huh?"

His smile is easy, disarming, and contagious. Beneath the lightness of his tone is a quiet authority that demands attention without raising his voice. Asa doesn't push; he doesn't have to. The weight of his presence does the work for him.

I cross my arms, standing still and watching him weave his charm. This is Asa in his element, exuding a calm that borders on invincibility. Moments ago, guests teetering on the edge of revolt now soften, their complaints fading as they lean into his charisma.

"My sincerest apologies for the disturbance," he continues, his hands moving gracefully like a conductor leading an orchestra. "To show our gratitude for your patience, how about a complimentary spa voucher for everyone here? On the house."

A ripple of murmured approval spreads through the crowd, the storm of discontent easing into a gentle tide. Asa flashes another smile, the kind that smooths over rough edges and turns chaos into compliance. Just like that, the tension dissipates, leaving behind the wreckage of Shana's outburst—and me.

I should feel relieved. I don't. If anything, the knots in my stomach pull tighter. As the foyer empties, the moment's weight presses harder against me. I'm not just the sister of the woman who caused this scene; I'm part of it. My family's shame is mine; my failure to contain it is a glaring reminder of everything I can't control.

"Sierra, you good?" Asa's voice breaks through my spiraling thoughts. He stands before me now; his brows pulled together in concern.

"Fine," I say automatically, the word brittle as it leaves my lips. It's a lie, and we both know it. My voice cracks under the strain of pretending I've got it all together. Protecting my family and preserving my reputation were the same thing. Now, they're tearing me apart.

Asa places a hand gently on my shoulder, his touch warm and calming. "Hey, we've got this," he says, his voice low and steady like he can make me believe it.

I want to laugh, to let the sharp edge of my dark humor cut through the tension. *Oh, we've definitely got something.* But the words stick in my throat. My family's dirty laundry isn't just out there—it's flapping in the Chesapeake Heights breeze for everyone to see.

"Thanks," I manage the word tight in my chest. My weak smile falters, and I know Asa sees through it.

"Sierra," he says again, his voice softer, his eyes meeting mine before looking at Jabari. "You're not alone in this. You're family now."

I nod, but as my gaze shifts to Amara, still leading Shana— my real family—down the corridor, her arm wrapped protectively around my sister, I feel the ache of solitude press against my chest. Deep down, no reassurance changes what I know: some battles aren't shared, no matter how much people want to help.

I go to them, and after she slips Shana through an office door, Amara's arms wrap around me, solid and unwavering, as the jasmine scent of her perfume cuts through the heaviness pressing on my chest. I finally let myself collapse into her embrace in the quiet hallway, far from the chaos and prying eyes. It feels safe here, in the circle of her arms, like the rest of the world can't touch me for just a moment.

"Everything is falling apart," I whisper, my voice muffled against her shoulder. The words feel like an admission of defeat, weighted with exhaustion, frustration, and the fear I've been too proud to name until now.

"Storms pass, Sierra," Amara says, her voice steady, each word deliberate. "And you're stronger than you think."

I laugh, the sound dry and brittle, cracking in the space between us. "Strong doesn't feel like enough right now," I admit, the vulnerability of the statement-making me wince.

"Strength isn't always a solo act," she replies gently, her arms tightening around me, grounding me. "It's okay to lean on others. Even Jabari."

Her words hit a nerve, and I pull back slightly, my expression guarded. "Jabari wants to fix things I'm not ready to hand over," I say, the words sharper than I intended.

Amara tilts her head, her expression softening with understanding. "Maybe so," she concedes, her tone as diplomatic as ever. "But his heart is in the right place, even if his methods are heavy-handed."

"Heavy-handed?" I snort softly, the faintest hint of a smile tugging at the corner of my mouth. "Feels more like a wrecking ball than a helping hand."

She laughs, her smile mirroring mine, though hers is laced with warmth and empathy. "Maybe. But he cares for you, Sierra. That counts for something, doesn't it?"

I sigh, my shoulders sagging under the weight of her question, under the truth of it. "It does," I admit, my voice barely above a whisper. "It scares me how much it does."

Amara's hand finds mine, squeezing gently. "Caring isn't a weakness, Sierra," she says, her voice soft but firm. "And letting someone care for you doesn't make you any less strong. You don't have to do this alone."

Her words sit heavy in the air, challenging the walls I've built around myself. I look away, my thoughts a tangled mess of what-ifs and fears I can't quite name. Because as much as I want to believe her, as much as I want to let Jabari in, the weight of letting go feels too risky. Too big. Too much.

"I'll think about it," I say finally, my voice tentative. It's not much, but it's all I can give her right now.

Amara nods, her smile softening. "That's a start."

Jabari stands across the hall from us like a sentinel, rigid and unyielding, as if bracing for a battle he knows he can't win. His hazel eyes, usually sharp and steady, are clouded with uncertainty—frustration, maybe, or regret. Either way, the sight of him, so solid and immovable, feels like a challenge I don't have the strength to face.

I feel his gaze on me, heavy and searching as if he's trying to piece me together while I fall apart. It sounds like the crowd has mostly dispersed now, Asa's charm smoothing over the edges of the chaos Shana left behind. But I'm still raw, still exposed, and Jabari? He's just standing there, his presence too big, intense, too... everything.

My heart twists in my chest, torn between the weight of his concern and the suffocating urge to push him away. I've been here before—a man trying to fix what they don't understand, thinking their money is the answer to all my problems. It isn't. It never is.

"Sierra," he starts, his voice low, hesitant. That alone feels like a betrayal. Jabari doesn't hesitate. He's decisive and deliberate, but now? Now he's off balance, and it's because of me.

I square my shoulders, forcing myself to meet his gaze even though I feel I'm coming undone beneath it. "I meant what I said earlier, Jabari. I need space," I say, the words more challenging to push out than expected. They sound cold, even to me, but I can't soften them. Not now.

His brow furrows, and for a moment, I see the flash of hurt he tries to hide. He steps forward, instinctively reaching for me, but then stops short, like he's run into an invisible wall. "Sierra, I—" His voice falters, and that crack in his armor almost undoes me.

"Please," I cut him off, my voice steadier this time, though my hands tremble. "Just... give me time."

The silence stretches between us, heavy and thick. He nods, his jaw tightening as his fists clench at his sides. "If that's what you need," he says, his voice clipped, his tone betraying the disappointment he's trying to hide.

I turn into the office, holding Shana before I can change my mind, before the pull of him, of us, becomes too much to resist. With every step I take, I feel the space between us growing—not just physically but in all the ways that matter. And it hurts. It hurts more than I expected.

When I finally stop, far enough away that I can't feel his eyes on me anymore, the air rushes out of me in a shaky breath. My sister is in a chair, mumbling something incoherent to herself while Amara rubs her back. She's having a mental breakdown, and the entire Freeman family is here to witness it. I lean against the cool wall, pressing my palms flat against it as if it can somehow hold me up when I feel like crumbling. I need to go over to her, but I can't. I just can't.

I should have never brought her here. What if they want her to be committed?

"Damn you, Jabari Freeman," I whisper, my voice laced with anger and something softer, something I don't want to name. "Why did you have to care so much?"

The words feel bitter on my tongue, but the truth behind them cuts even deeper. He cares—too much, too intensely— and that scares me. Because as much as I want to push him away, a small, fragile part of me wants to lean into him, to let him carry some of the weight that's been crushing me for so long.

I close my eyes, trying to steady the storm raging inside me. "You can do this, Sierra," I whisper, shaky but resolute. "You've handled worse."

And I have. But somehow, this feels different. The stakes feel higher, the potential for heartbreak sharper. Because it's not just about fixing Shana's mess or keeping up appearances anymore. It's about Jabari. About us. About the possibility of something real, something I might not be ready for.

But even as I tell myself I need space, I know the truth: I'm not just trying to protect myself. I'm trying to protect him— from me, this mess, the weight of everything I carry. Because if I let him in and let myself fall, I'm not sure we will ever recover.

TWENTY-TWO

After the Love Is Gone

JABARI

TWO WEEKS LATER

I stare at the numbers on the latest hotel chain buyout offer, the digits blurring together like a language I don't understand. None of it makes sense because all I see is her face. Sierra's face—the way it scrunches up like a bunny when she laughs, that fierce determination that lights up her eyes when she's hell-bent on proving me wrong.

Two weeks. Two damn weeks of polite smiles and shallow small talk that feels like eating dry, unseasoned food. Unsatisfying, bland, and maddeningly wrong. She asked for space—*space*—like we're teenagers caught in some summer fling instead of two grown adults who should know better. I agreed with her plan to save this place and breathe life into the resort without submitting to corporate overlords. But I didn't sign up for this distance, this strained silence between us.

It also doesn't help that I spent teh last week keeping my foot on Jackson Taylor's neck. My surveillance caught him sneaking around Sierra's sister Shana's place. So, my brothers and I paid him a special visit to drop off a dossier of information.

We had everything on him, down to the brand of drawers the man wore.

We came strapped up in case he tried anything stupid.

He didn't, and I think he knows I'm not bluffing. I will end him and his family if he fucks with me or mine.

Now, if I could only get "mine" to talk to me.

"Jabari, what the hell are you doing?" Malik's voice slices through my fog like a machete through tall grass. He barges into my office, his energy bristling with judgment, and slams a copy of the offer onto my desk like it personally insulted him.

"You gonna sell out our history for this?" he growls, his disdain palpable. It lands like spit on my father's memory, and for a second, I see red.

I stand slowly, muscles coiled with frustration. "You think this is easy for me?" My voice is low, sharp with barely contained anger. Malik always knows how to push my buttons, and today he's hitting every damn one. He pisses me off with his holier-than-thou attitude. Why don't we know where he was the three years before he was discharged from the Rangers? How about we lay his sins and shortcomings out for everyone to see?

He meets my glare, unflinching, but there's a catch of caution in his eyes. *Smart man.* He backs off just enough to take some of the bite out of his tone. "Look, I get it. You've got a lot on your plate. And Sierra's got you twisted in knots. But stop crying over her like some lovesick fool. If you want the woman, then get her. Fight for her. Like you fought for everything else in your life." He gestures to the medals and plaques on my office wall as proof I once believed that I could fix anything.

"Ha!' I scoff. You're one to talk. I heard Jade just returned from her vacation; I bet you spent your night watching her cottage from that surveillance suite you keep in your basement." Malik's clenched fists are the only indication that I surprised him. "You didn't know I knew about that, did you? I make it my business to know everything. So why don't you take some of your own advice and claim your woman before you're arrested for stalking."

" You don't know what you're talking about," he bites out. "I'm just trying to keep her safe."

I roll my eyes. "From who? You?"

"No, you asshole. From... You know what, never mind. This isn't about me. It's obvious you love Sierra, and she digs you too. Just handle it."

"Thanks for the pep talk," I say dryly, sarcasm dripping from every syllable. It takes everything in me not to leap across the desk and knock some humility into him. "I'll keep that in mind."

"Man up, Jabari." His eyes blaze, the stubborn Freeman fire burning bright. "This is bigger than you and Sierra. This is about our legacy. You need her, and we do, too."

"Legacy," I echo, the word bitter in my mouth. The weight of it presses down on me, heavy as the name I carry. The Freemans' legacy isn't just about this resort; it's about our family, our history, our damn identity.

"Damn straight," Malik snaps, oblivious to the war waging inside me. "Now, make the right choice."

Before I can respond, he storms out, leaving behind a trail of indignation. I take a deep breath, but it doesn't help. The pressure refuses to ease.

The door swings open again and in strides Amara, her presence both soothing and electrifying. "You're not seriously considering this offer, are you?" she demands, her voice sharp and commanding. "We can't sell. This isn't just land and buildings, Jabari—it's our soul."

I lean back in my chair, regarding her with admiration and weariness. Amara has always been the rock in our family, the one who holds firm no matter how rough the storm. Her unshakable conviction and her passion for Chesapeake Heights are fierce enough to make history books.

"Amara, it's not that simple," I say, my tone clipped. But before I can explain, she cuts me off.

"It is that simple," she counters, her words like cannon fire. "We owe it to our ancestors to preserve this place. To our kids. To everyone who looks to us and sees strength, resilience, pride."

Her gaze locks on to mine, unyielding, and I feel the pull of her conviction. She's right. Deep down, I know she's right. But knowing it doesn't make it easier.

"All right," I say finally, surrendering with my hands. I stand and walk around to lean against my desk. "But how can we make it all make financial sense? This offer will keep our children, grandchildren, and great-grandchildren wealthy. We can't forget that our generations also need to eat. Laurels won't keep anyone dry during a storm."

I look behind Amara and glimpse Sierra's silhouette hovering through the half-open door in the hallway. My breath catches. She's standing there, arms wrapped around herself like she's holding something fragile together. The sight of her twists something within me, a feeling I can't shake. Guilt? Longing? Both?

This is so stupid

She's listening. I can see it in how her posture stiffens, and her fingers grip her arms as she braces for a blow. I can practically hear her thoughts and see the guilt and frustration etched on her face. She's blaming herself for the delays, the mess Shana dragged us into, and for everything.

"Sierra," I whisper, the word slipping out like a prayer she'll never hear. She doesn't move or look in, but I know she's there, caught between staying and running. Always on the edge of retreat.

"Jabari?" Amara's voice snaps me back to the moment, her brow raised in expectation.

"Right," I mutter, dragging my focus back to her. "We'll fight for it. For Chesapeake Heights, whatever we do has to make financial sense, Amara. I promise to work on it." The words are firm and resolute. Because that's what Freemans do— we fight. Against odds, against nature, against each other if we must.

Amara nods, "Don't be afraid to engage Sierra in this. She had wonderful ideas. After all, it was her that got us on the same page. She's not going to come to you, Bari; she's too scared and too damn prideful for that. You're going to have to do it." Satisfied that she's bossed me around enough for the day, she leaves with determination, radiating from every click of her heels like a beacon.

But my eyes linger on the door, catching the faintest whisper of movement as Sierra slips away.

One thing becomes clear as I sit there: the papers have been forgotten on my desk. If fighting for this resort means fighting for her, too, I'm ready. I'm done waiting, done playing it safe.

She wants space? Fine. But space doesn't mean surrender. It's time to stop standing on the sidelines and show Sierra exactly how far I wi

TWENTY-THREE

Time Will Reveal

SIERRA

THE DOOR TO MY OFFICE CREAKS OPEN, AND EVEN before I hear her voice, I know it's Tiana. She always enters a room like she owns the place, her energy unapologetically bold, impossible to miss. Her presence is a mix of no-nonsense authority and the kind of warmth you don't realize you need until it snatches you and your edges together.

Today, though, her arrival feels like an interruption and a lifeline.

She insisted we have lunch together today at the Chesapeake Heights Clubhouse, claiming she hadn't seen it yet and wanted to "scope out my kingdom." I agreed half-heartedly, distracted by the growing mountain of problems. Now she's caught me mid-crisis, my gaze fixed on the corporate hotel chain buyout offer spread across my desk like it holds all the answers to a test I'm failing.

"You know," she starts, her voice cutting through the thick fog of my thoughts, "you might've said yes to lunch, but sitting here brooding doesn't count as keeping your word." Her heels click against the polished floor as she steps closer, her sharp eyes narrowing as she takes in my slumped posture. "What are you even doing?"

"Thinking," I mutter without looking up, though the word doesn't quite capture the spiral I'm caught in. It feels more like drowning. The numbers on the offer blur together as guilt, frustration, and something that feels suspiciously like longing churn in my chest.

It's an eight-figure deal. Enough to tempt anyone. It's enough to make me understand why Jabari's even considering it. But he'll regret it if he goes through with it—I know he will. I wish I could talk to him, but he's been avoiding me, and I can't blame him.

Sometimes, I linger outside his office, hoping he'll notice me and give me one of those steady, knowing looks that always sets me on edge in the best way. But he never does, and every time I walk away, I feel like a coward.

"Thinking or sulking?" Tiana presses, perching on the edge of my desk with the grace that makes even her most exasperated moments look poised. "Because I'm not here to watch you wallow, Sierra."

"I'm not wallowing," I snap, though the bite in my tone is half-hearted at best. "I'm strategizing."

"Strategizing, huh?" She leans forward, crossing her arms over her chest, her tone laced with skepticism. "You look like someone who's been staring at the same problem for so long you've convinced yourself it's unsolvable."

I glance at her, the concern in her dark eyes only adding to the knot in my chest. "It feels like it is," I admit softly, the words slipping out before I can stop them. "The resort, Jabari... everything's slipping through my fingers."

Her expression shifts, sharpening like the edge of a blade. "Jabari?" she repeats, her voice low, steady, and dangerous in the way only a best friend's can be. "That man loves you, and you're throwing it all away because of some misplaced guilt. Do you think your sister feels guilty for even one second about what she's done to you? No. So why are you carrying her mistakes like they're your cross to bear?"

"Because she's my *sister*!" The words rip out of me like a wound torn open, raw, and bleeding. I push myself to my feet, the chair screeching against the floor as I rise. "You don't get it, Tiana. You don't have to pick up the pieces every damn time someone else's decisions blow up in your face!"

Tiana doesn't flinch or move an inch as I stand there trembling, my voice echoing down the quiet hallway. Instead, she rises slowly, her expression softening in the way only she can manage—firm but compassionate, unyielding but kind.

"Sierra." Her voice is low, steady as a heartbeat, and she pulls me into her arms before I can protest. Her hold is firm, grounding me like roots in the earth. "Breathe," she says softly. "It's time to exhale. You couldn't save your mom from that sickness, and you can't save Shana from herself. You've got to let this go."

The dam breaks. The tears come fast and hard, soaking her shoulder as my body shakes with sobs I've been holding back for far too long. "I don't know how to let go, Ti," I whisper, the words muffled against her shoulder. "I don't know how."

"You will," she murmurs, stroking my back in soothing circles. "And you don't have to figure it out alone. We'll do it together. You hear me? Together."

Through blurry eyes, I see movement at the far end of the hallway. Ann Freeman steps into view, her heels clicking softly against the floor as she approaches. Even in the shadows, her presence commands the space. She doesn't speak immediately, simply watching us with those piercing eyes that seem to see right through the walls I've spent years building.

Her tone is calm, authoritative, and final when she speaks. "I'm calling a meeting," she announces, her words cutting through the silence like a knife. It's time we address this head-on as a family."

"But I'm not fam—" I start to protest, but she silences me with a sharp look, one brow arched in a way that brooks no argument.

"Nonsense," she says firmly. "You've been part of this family since you stepped foot in this resort. I want both of you in the family room now."

Facing Jabari right now feels like walking into a fire I'm not ready for. My stomach twists, dread coiling low and tight, but there's also something else—a faint spark of hope. Ann Freeman doesn't waste words; when she calls a meeting, it's not to rehash problems. It's to solve them. If anyone can bring this fractured family back together, it's her. And if I can help her do that, maybe there's still hope for Jabari and me.

I step back from Tiana, wiping my tear-streaked face with trembling hands. My voice wavers but doesn't break. "Let's do this."

Tiana smiles, a look of pride softening her features. "That's my girl."

I take a shaky breath and follow Ann down the hallway, each step feeling heavier than the last. I don't know if I'm ready to face Jabari—hell, I'm probably not—but I'll do it anyway. For the Freemans. For Chesapeake Heights.

For us.

* * *

Baycrest's family room feels heavier tonight. It's usually a place of warmth, where laughter bounces off the walls, and the faint scent of beeswax polish mingles with the memories etched into every corner. But tonight, it's a battleground. The soft glow of the lamps does little to soften the tension in the air. I sit on the couch, my nerves frayed and my thoughts tangled in knots, as Ann steps forward to command the room. Her presence is unshakable, a lighthouse cutting through the fog of our collective uncertainty.

"Thank you all for coming," she begins, calm but purposeful. "This resort has weathered many storms, from nature and from within. Now, we face another turning point. It's an eight-figure turning point, to be exact. It's time to share what's in our hearts about the path forward without judgment."

I glance at Jabari, seated at the far end of the room, his posture rigid, his jaw tight. He doesn't look at me. He never does anymore. The distance between us feels more expansive than ever, and I don't know how to broach it. Maybe I can't.

Asa stands, drawing the room's attention. His usual easy charm is dimmed tonight, and his smile lacks its usual luster. He clears his throat, his hand brushing the back of his neck, and the vulnerability in the gesture tugs at something deep inside me.

"I've been thinking," he starts, his voice steady but low, like he's choosing every word carefully. "About this place—our legacy. We've got roots here deeper than the ocean, but that doesn't pay the bills or fix the damage from past storms."

He pauses, his gaze sweeping the room, landing briefly on each of us. "Maybe it's foolish to turn down a sure thing for a dream that feels more and more like chasing shadows. But"—he hesitates, his voice thick with the weight of the moment—"then I see the fire in y'all's eyes, and I wonder if maybe those shadows are worth chasing after all. But at the end of the day, it always comes right back to the money. We could be set for life with a deal like this."

His words hang in the air, heavy and raw, and the room falls silent. Ann nods, her lips pressed together in acknowledgment, but she doesn't speak. She lets us all sit with the weight of Asa's confession, and I feel it—thick and unrelenting, pressing down on all of us.

The air shifts as Amara rises, the firelight casting her in hues of gold and amber. Her voice is steady and unwavering. "This place," she begins, her eyes scanning the room before landing on mine, "is more than land and buildings—it's our heritage. Our ancestors built Chesapeake Heights with their sweat and dreams. We can't measure that in dollars."

"Tell 'em, Mara," Malik mutters from his shadow, his usual bravado tempered into something softer.

I cross my arms over my chest, leaning back in my seat, trying to mask the turbulence churning in my gut. But I can't stop the memories from surfacing. Jabari told me how he loved to see his dad's hands, rough and callused, as he rebuilt houses on the property after storms. I hear his voice, full of quiet determination, promising me that he would be as good a man as his father was because he wouldn't allow anything to shake the foundation of this family.

Amara's voice pulls me back to the present. "Jabari," she says, her gaze locking on her brother. "Remember when we were kids and Dad had us plant those saplings after the storm? He said we were sowing hope."

Asa scoffs, "Hope doesn't have a damn balance sheet."

Amara turns her gaze to him, her expression calm but resolute. "Neither does legacy, Asa," she counters. Her words are challenging, her conviction a riptide visibly tugging at Asa's defenses. "We're the caretakers of something irreplaceable. We owe it to future generations to preserve the soul of Chesapeake Heights."

Her words land like stones in my chest, and I look away, my

gaze settling on the flickering fire instead. The room feels like it's waiting, balanced on the edge of a knife, every breath held as if we're all afraid to tip it one way or the other.

Finally, Jabari stands, his height casting a long shadow across the room. His voice is low, filled with exhaustion. "Fine," he says, the word clipped but certain. "I'll dismiss the offer. But Sierra must help me secure the Historical Society Landmark Grant if we're doing this. Otherwise, we won't be able to pull this off.

He turns to me with a gaze that looks right into my soul. "All-in Sierra, no half measures."

"Always," I reply before addressing the people who have slowly become my family. "Look, I know I'm not blood," I fight to keep my voice steady despite the tremor of my hands. "But this place... It's more than just a job for me. It's a symbol. A legacy of hope and resilience for the community, for us. I won't let you down." I look over to Ann, and her smile is small but triumphant. When she nods, I take my seat.

I glance back at Jabari, but he doesn't meet my eyes. Instead, he focuses on the family and the future they're all fighting to protect. Instantly, I feel like an outsider, caught in the push and pull of belonging and isolation. My heart aches for him, us, and the distance I created but don't know how to bridge.

But as I sit there, listening to the quiet hum of voices rising again, I make a silent promise. I'll fight, not just for the Landmark grant, but to prove that I can be more than the chaos that followed me here.

I will show Jabari that the space I asked for wasn't about pushing him away but finding a way to come back stronger.

TWENTY-FOUR

I Can't Tell You Why

JABARI

IF IT'S NOT ONE THING, IT'S ANOTHER.

Two days ago, I survived the family meeting. Barely. But it wasn't a loss. I managed to secure Sierra's partnership in working toward the resort gaining landmark status with the Maryland State Historical Society—a perfect excuse to keep her close. To step back into her orbit. I want to remind her and myself that whatever distance she puts between us, I'm not going anywhere. I've been good—respectful of her boundaries —for two weeks. But I'm over it. I want her, and I will have her.

Not today, though.

Today, the entire resort and town are bracing for a tropical storm less than an hour away. The winds are already making themselves known, and Chesapeake Heights is on alert. Every-one, including Sierra, is in GO mode, preparing for the storm's possible wrath.

I'm outside, double-checking the lines of sandbags at the resort's entrance when the first whip of wind strikes hard enough to knock me back a step. The gust carries the sharp, salty promise of what's coming. The Chesapeake Heights Bay Resort is more than just a building; it's our historical monument. And I'll be damned if I let a storm tear down what my ancestors built.

"Jabari, are those sandbags high enough?" Amir shouts, his voice barely carrying over the roar of the wind.

"Higher than your sense of humor, brother," I snap back, though the banter feels hollow.

I look over my shoulder and smile at my techie brother, who is more comfortable in his bespoke suits and behind a computer than out here in the elements. But he's a Freeman and does his part and wouldn't have it any other way. I do wish he'd put on the rain boots I offered him. Those Jordans he's wearing will be ruined in this sand and rain. Sierra nicknamed him Pretty Boy Blue because of his penchant for Tom Ford Navy Suits and matching Nike Jordans. I can't believe he lets her get away with it.

I shove aside the thoughts of Sierra that won't stop circling. Her laughter, her voice, even her damn freckles—all of it haunts me more than the storm bearing down on us.

"Bari, focus," I mutter, shaking my head as I shift my attention to the task at hand. I stalk back toward the main hall, where Sierra orchestrates the guest evacuation. If there's one thing she excels at, it's creating calm out of chaos. And yet, seeing her there, clipboard in hand, commanding the room with that quiet, unshakable authority, only throws me further off balance.

Her voice cuts through the noise like an anchor. "We're moving the last of the guests to the clubhouse and Baycrest now," she says, directing staff and reassuring guests with practiced ease. She looks steady and composed, but I see the tremor in her fingers when she checks her clipboard. *She's exhausted.* No one else would notice, but I do.

"Sierra, update?" I ask, my tone colder than I intend, but I don't trust myself to say more. I want to demand she go upstairs and rest. But I know that won't go over well.

She doesn't look at me; she focuses on her task. "We're almost done here," she says briskly, her professionalism as sharp as a blade.

"Good," I reply, though the word feels heavier than it should, weighted with everything unsaid between us.

I should tell her how proud I am. Watching her take charge like this makes my chest swell. I should hold her, tell her I've missed her every second these past two weeks. But instead, I stand there like a damn statue, letting the chill of our interactions freeze me in place.

She moves through the room like a commander on the front line, her freckled face calm and collected as she offers reassurance to guests. But I see how her shoulders tense when I get too close, the hitch in her step when my presence becomes unavoidable. We're both feeling it, this tension strung tight between us. It's a script neither of us wants to play out, but here we are, stuck reciting lines full of barbed words and unspoken truths.

"Keep everyone calm," I say, forcing my voice into a neutral command.

"That's me, the queen of calm," she retorts, her words dripping with a dark humor that doesn't reach her eyes.

I hesitate, then give in to the traitorous impulse to speak. "Be safe, Sierra," I say, my soft tone betraying me.

"Of course," she fires back, her voice taking on a softer tone as well.

I turn before I can say more, my footsteps heavy as I head

back into the storm. But as I glance over my shoulder, I catch her profile—strong yet vulnerable in a way that unravels me. She's everything I admire, wrapped in a contradiction that leaves me wanting her more than my next breath.

The storm outside rages as I step into its chaos, but it's nothing compared to the one she stirs in me. I face the elements with the same resolve I've used to bury my feelings for her. Control—over love, over weather—might be an illusion, but it's all I have to hold on to right now.

And I'll be damned if I let either one sweep me away.

I'm outside, rain soaking through my clothes as I secure the last shutters. Every slam of wood against the frame feels like defiance, an answer to the storm's fury. But as I push the final latch into place, the sound of tires crunching through rising floodwaters pulls my attention to the driveway.

A black SUV lurches toward the entrance, its headlights slicing through the chaos. My gut tightens. I know an armored SUV when I see one, and it's sporting diplomatic plates. The storm outside is bad enough; the last thing we need is VIP guests right now. I didn't look at the guest ledger this week, but I know who this could be. After all, I invited them. I didn't expect them so soon.

"Jabari!" Sierra's voice cuts through the howling wind. I turn, and there she is, clipboard clutched to her chest like it's the only thing tethering her to the ground. Even soaked to the bone, she's gorgeous, the wind whipping her curls into a wild halo around her face. "We've got more guests—diplomatic travelers! I just got the call..." I follow her gaze to the SUV as its doors swing open.

Yep, I'm one step ahead of you, babe.

A couple steps out, arms locked around each other like they can ward off the storm with their unity alone. When I see them, there's no doubt who they are; it's Maya and Adom Annan.

Adom is a powerful Ashanti Chief. My SEAL unit helped him and his brother, Senya—an Ashanti Prince—rescue Senya's wife from a sex-trafficking Trokosi temple in Ghana. I also met his supermodel-turned-diplomat wife, who handled the after-care for the other girls we rescued that day. She's also a professor whose work I respect. Together, they portray something I've spent years avoiding: love that stands unbroken against all odds.

They may also help us save this resort. Maya is influential in historical circles. But I don't want anyone to know I brought them here, as that would raise too many questions.

"That's Maya Annan," Sierra shouts, her voice barely reaching me over the howl of the wind. I've seen her in fashion magazines and on society pages! But what are they doing here?"

I lie easily. "She's conducting research for a new book on the history of the Black Elite—she wants to see our archives. They've been in DC this past week and decided to come here today. Maya has a deadline that she can't miss."

The Annans move toward us, their faces calm but determined. Even as the rain lashes their skin and the wind tugs at their coats, they seem untouchable, like their connection is armor. They lean on each other, every step a testament to something unshakable.

I don't miss how Sierra's eyes linger on their clasped hands. Her gaze softens for just a moment, but it's enough. I catch the flicker of longing there, and it twists something inside me—a sharp, unwanted pang of jealousy that I bury deep.

"Come," I call out, motioning for them to follow. "Welcome to Chesapeake Heights."

"Thank you," Maya says, her voice cutting through the chaos with gratitude. Adom grabs my hand and gives me a firm handshake. We can't discuss the mission we served with outsiders, so the Annans and I must keep our affiliation a secret. Adom nods, giving me a silent greeting, and keeps his expression steady even as the storm threatens to consume everything around us. They move purposefully, as though they've done this before—weathered storms and come out stronger.

"Sierra, go inside and make sure they're comfortable," I say, my tone gruff. It's not doubt in her abilities that makes my voice sharp—it never is. It's the surge of protectiveness rising within me, fierce and unbidden. I need her inside and out of these elements. She doesn't need my protection, I remind myself. But that doesn't stop the instinct from clawing at me.

"Yes, sir," she replies, throwing the words over her shoulder as she leads the Annans into the lobby. Her tone is casual, even playful, but her smile doesn't reach her eyes. It hasn't for weeks. Regardless, hearing her call me sir makes my dick hard.

"Be careful," I growl, the words slipping out before I can stop them. My voice is rougher than intended, and my need is too raw.

I stand there momentarily, letting the rain pummel me as I watch her go. Every fiber of my being wants to follow her, to grab her hand the way Adom does Maya's, to pull her close and tell her how much she means to me. To shield her from the storm—not just this one, but any that come.

But instead, I stand back, letting her go. This is the control I cling to—the only thing that keeps the raw edges of my soul from bleeding out.

As we head back inside Baycrest, the storm rages harder. It embodies the turmoil inside me, reflecting the battle I wage within. Sierra is the eye of my hurricane, the calm, and the catalyst.

TWENTY-FIVE
Kiss You All Over

SIERRA

ONCE I SETTLED THE ANNANS, I NEEDED A BREAK from all the employee questions and guest requests.

Hell, I needed a break from Jabari.

I want to jump his bones every time he's near, and I'm getting desperate. I need to go ahead and tell the man I'm sorry for pushing him away so we can get on with the make-up portion of our roller-coaster ride.

Needing coffee, I head to the break room downstairs and find myself drawn to the voices trickling from inside. The door is ajar, spilling a sliver of light and fragments of conversation into the dim corridor. Malik's voice snags my attention first—a low rumble that holds the weight of concern.

"Man, you think Jabari is gonna go through with it? Head back to VA Beach?" Malik asks, his words laden with a brotherly mix of disbelief and curiosity.

"Looks like it," Amir replies, his tone carrying the resignation of someone who had plans laid out and now watches them crumble. "He was talking about needing a reset, a fresh start or something."

His words slice through me like shards of glass. My mind vividly imagines Jabari packing up that black beast of a truck and driving off, leaving Chesapeake Heights—and me—in his rearview mirror. A surge of betrayal swells within me, laced with a bitter sting of abandonment.

"Damn," Malik mutters. "After everything that's happened..."

"Life goes on, right?" Amir interjects, a note of forced cheerfulness threading through his words." We devised a plan to keep Chesapeake Heights afloat, thanks to Sierra. I'm sure he'll return to VA Beach once he gets that plan off the ground. It's not like he doesn't still work for the government on that base. What does he do, train SEALS now?"

Malik snorts. "Yeah, right. That dude is on some Black Ops shit. I saw him giving all kinds of signals and head nods to that Ashanti chief who arrived today. That's why I got out of the Rangers. It was too many secrets and not enough support when you survive. We can kill insurgents, but the moment you pop a cap in a negroe's ass over here that deserves it, they wanna throw a fit. The shit I ..."

The conversation fades as they move away, leaving an echo of their words hanging in the air like a bad omen. I lean against the wall, feeling its coldness seep through my damp polo, mirroring the chill settling in my heart.

I can't even deal with the fact that I think Malik is about to confess some murderous shit to his brother; nope, all I can think about is, *How can Jabari leave?*

I shake my head, trying to dispel the hurt that threatens to engulf me. He doesn't owe me anything. After all, I'm the one that pushed him away. But if what Malik said was true, he would always go back. All those sweet words, the grand gestures, none of it matters. Because he never told me he'd stay. Shit, I never even asked.

I knew this would end in heartbreak one way or the other.

The sound of my name snaps me back to reality. I plaster on a smile and stride toward the source, burying the hurt deep down where it can't distract me from the tasks at hand.

Jabari towers in the command center, orchestrating the staff with a calm that belies the chaos swirling outside. His gaze flicks across the monitors, each screen showing the resort bracing against nature's fury.

"All right, everyone, listen up!" Jabari's clear and authoritative voice slices through the commotion. "We've got to double-check all the guest homes and ensure no one's left behind before this storm hits full force."

His eyes are hawk-like as they scan the room, missing nothing. With each report that comes in—secure windows, reinforced doors, emergency supplies distributed—his nod is firm, appreciative of the staff's diligence.

"Jabari, the eastern wing's generator is acting up," one of the maintenance guys reports, rushing over with urgency creased into his brow.

"Show me," Jabari commands, stepping away from the hub with a purposeful stride. In moments like these, he's in his element—a leader fortified by adversity, each decision a testament to his commitment to safeguarding every soul under his watch. There is no room for hesitation, no space for personal turmoil.

As he navigates the halls with deliberate steps, his every action speaks of devotion—not to a place but to a legacy, to the people who call this resort home, even if only for a night. Unbeknownst to him, my heart is caught in a maelstrom of misunderstanding while he remains anchored in the duty that defines him.

I should do the same.

The lights flicker, a sputtering prelude to darkness. "Damn," I mutter as the room plunges into darkness without a whisper of warning. Jabari's silhouette is a towering shadow against the emergency lights' feeble glow.

"Where's the backup generator?" he barks, his voice a force that seems to propel the maintenance crew into action. I trail behind him, my mind a whirlpool of mismatched thoughts, churning with the chaos of the storm and the turmoil within.

His long strides eat up the distance to the eastern wing, his movements sure, calculated—the man is all Navy SEAL, muscles coiled and ready. He doesn't miss a beat or pause to consider the possibility of retreat. Yet, here I am, drowning in a sea of doubt, clutching at the debris of Malik's words that hinted at Jabari's departure.

"Hand me the flashlight," he demands, his hand outstretched without looking back as if he knows I'll be there. I hand it over, our fingers brushing in the dark—a spark in the void. The silent exchange crackles in the air, a current charging through me, reminding me of what I fear losing.

"Got it!" Jabari exclaims with a grunt, the sound of metal clanging, his resourcefulness on full display as he wrestles life back into the generator: the power surges, lights blooming like a promise across the resort. Right now, he is triumphant in restoring the resort's power. He doesn't look like a man plotting his escape back to Virginia Beach. *But what do I know?*

"Good work, Freeman," I say, forcing a smile as I step away, putting distance between us because proximity to Jabari is a hazard. If he's leaving soon, I must maintain the distance between us.

"Sierra," he calls out, and I pause, feeling his gaze heavy on my back. "Everything okay?"

"Of course," I lie, my laugh sharp enough to cut glass. "Just another day at Chesapeake Heights, right? Managing tropical tempests and faulty generators."

"Right," he replies, and I hear his disbelief in that word.

I slip away to the solitude of my office. If only our hearts had a generator to kick them back to life, to light up the corners darkened by betrayal and doubt.

Because as the wind howls a mournful tune, I can't shake the feeling that we are both waiting for a rescue that may never come.

* * *

"Hi, Sierra," Jade, the events director, greets me as she peeks into my office.

I'm so grateful we became fast friends when I arrived at Baycrest on my first workday. She's been an absolute lifesaver.

She'd been on vacation for the last two weeks, and I'd missed her.

We had breakfast this morning, and she opened up a bit and told me that she shares her little girl with an abusive ex-husband, who's now locked up where he should be. That was a shock, but we bonded over our resilience to trauma.

"We just got a report that a family may still be hunkered down in the Bayshore house. I can't find Jabari anywhere. Have you seen him?"

Yep. I'm practically stalking him.

I nod. "I know where he is, girl; I'll get word to him."

"I figured you would know where he's hiding if no one else did." She giggles, and I roll my eyes and laugh. "All right, girl, I'm around if you need anything. She runs out, and I stand.

Jabari is still in the Command Center, trying to keep the resort's power on and stable. I don't want to disturb him, so I quickly walk by and decide to check on the Bayshore house myself.

When I look outside, I see the storm has picked up considerably since I was last outside. I shrug on my raincoat, zipping it over unsteady heartbeats. I'll check and make sure the house is empty. If it's not, then I'll radio Jabari for support.

Malik comes around the corner, chatting and smiling with Jade. *Interesting.* He sees me suiting up and gently turns away from Jade to fuss at me. "Sierra, I know you're not considering going out in this weather."

I give him an exhausted look. "Listen, I'm just going to check on the Bayshore home. Jade told me a family might have hunkered down there against our evacuation orders."

Malik crosses his arms across his chest. I never noticed how many tattoos he had before. His arms are covered them. "I know; Jade told me. She also said that she told you, and you told her you would let Jabari know so he could handle it."

He looks around. "As a matter of fact, where's Jabari? Does he know you're heading outside?"

"I don't need his permission." I snap without breaking stride.

I push through the front door and resist the storm swallowing me whole.

I make it about ten feet before I hear him behind me.

"Sierra!" His voice cuts through the tempest. I spin around, squinting into the onslaught, and there he is—Jabari, big as the storm itself, bearing down on me with eyes fiercer than any gale.

"Jabari, go back! I've got this!"

"Like hell you do!" His voice is almost lost to the wind, but his meaning is clear.

We reach Bayshore House together, and I fumble with the keys, cursing the trembling in my fingers. When I finally open the door, I call out. "Hello! Is anyone here?"

Jabari pushes past me and mumbles, "It looks empty, but I'll check upstairs."

I don't respond; instead, I go deeper into the house. A crack of thunder falls, darkness falls like a curtain, the power snuffed out by nature's breath. I yelp, more from surprise than fear, but it's enough.

"Sierra!" Jabari's arms close around me, pulling me away from the imagined abyss.

"Damn it, Jabari! I'm fine," I snap, my voice betraying the relief of his touch.

"Fine? You call this fine?" He shakes me gently, his frustration palpable. "You shouldn't have tried to come out here alone."

"Neither should you." It's a weak comeback, drenched in hypocrisy, and we both know it.

His scowl softens, and suddenly, our faces are inches apart, breaths mingling in the charged air between us. "You're driving me crazy, Siren."

"And you're a liar," I scream. You said you wanted me, but you're leaving. You're returning to Virginia, to your perfect military life, and leaving the crazy Siren here alone."

He sighs in frustration. "What are you talking about Sierra? I haven't made any decisions about anything like that. Shit! I've been too focused on getting you to talk to me for the past two weeks. I've been going insane not being able to talk to you or touch you. Don't you get it? Baby, you're it for me."

"What?" I mumble. "But—"

And then his lips are on mine, demanding, insistent, a gale-force wind of their own. My protests die on a moan as I kiss him back, for all his fine ass is worth. My thoughts are lost to the feel of his hard body, the strength of his arms, and the relentless drumming of the rain against the roof. Love and desire tangle together, fierce as the rainstorm outside.

When we pull apart, we look into each other's eyes with hard breaths and beating hearts. No one has to say a thing; we know what we both want and want it now.

Jabari lifts me and carries me to the nearest couch without a preamble. He sits me down before standing up and wordlessly stripping off his wet clothing. He gives me a fierce look, telling me I should get about the business of doing the same.

I mirror his movements. He kicks his shoes and socks off. I toe mine off. He rips his coat and jacket off. I rip mine off. He unbuckles his belt and swiftly lowers his jeans and boxers, and I do the same. I lift my hips and peel the wet, sticky khakis off along with my black lace thong until I'm sitting on these people's ivory suede couch, butt-ass naked and dripping wet.

When I look up, his beautiful Black dick is staring me straight in the face as he stands before me, and I can't resist any longer. I lean forward and inhale the warm, hard flesh as far as I can down my throat until I choke. And then I slide back up his shaft, dragging my tongue underneath until I hear him cuss me out.

"Fuck, Sierra!" He looks down at me like he's in pain and wants to cry. "Siren, that shit feels so good; you're gonna turn me into a screaming little bitch."

I don't take my eyes off him as I slide right back down his dick like it's the only thing that's keeping me tethered to this moment. When I find my rhythm, it's a wrap. Up and down, I go on his dick, taking as much of him as I can into the back of my throat with each pass.

He's enormous, and I know I'll never be able to swallow all of it, but I'm greedy, so I try my hardest. I use my hands and lubricate them with the saliva I left behind before licking his tip and massaging his balls.

Then he shouts and holds the back of my head and fucks

my mouth like I know he's going to destroy my pussy once I finish sucking out his soul.

"That's my good girl, Siren. Yeah, let me fuck that pretty mouth just... like...

Thi—" Before he can finish talking shit, his cum shoots down my throat like a jet headed for landing. I swallow every single drop until my big, strong man is weak in the knees. When I pop off his dick and lick my fingers and the corners of my mouth clean, he stumbles a bit before taking a few deep breaths and coming back to earth with a look of pure determination on his face.

I don't get to say anything; I'm lifted and manhandled in the best way. He throws me over the arm of the couch, then my ass is in the air, and he slaps it three times before pushing straight into my pussy with no mercy.

"Ahhh, Bari!" I scream and try to scoot away, but he only slaps my ass again and growls.

"Naww, Siren. Don't try to run away from this dick now. You talked all that shit with your eyes, tongue, and mouth on my dick a few minutes ago. You are getting all nine of these inches until you cream all over my dick."

His pace is relentless, and he gives me no quarter to brace myself. So, the only thing I can do is relax and let my arms rest in front of me while he blows my back out, and I love every single screaming minute of it. It doesn't take long before I'm crashing, cursing, and creaming all over his dick, just like he said I would.

"That's right, Siren. Give it to me. Give Daddy all your cum. Squeeze me just like that."

He follows right behind me with a growl and a bite to my shoulder before collapsing on top of me. His heaviness is the security blanket I never knew I needed.

After we catch our breath, he gently lifts me and lays us

both on the giant couch. He spoons behind me, and I swear I feel his dick harden again.

I laugh as I rub my ass against him. "Already Jabari, really?"

He grunts. "Hell yeah, you kept my pussy from me for two weeks, I'm about to fuck your brains out until this storm passes. Is that all right with you, Siren?"

I open my legs wide enough for his dick to hit my entrance and moan.

"Yes sir, That's all right with me."

TWENTY-SIX

Just Once

JABARI

THE CALM AFTER A STORM ALWAYS BLOWS ME.

Eight hours ago, I would have sworn the rain and wind would never stop. And that when it did, nothing on our part of the Earth would be the same.

For me, it's better because I'm still here, with Sierra wrapped around me, her warm skin pressed against mine, her breath a steady rhythm against my chest. I'm naked, tangled, and untethered from the world beyond this room.

"Think anyone noticed we're missing?" Her smothered voice is playful and low, vibrating against my skin like the hum of a song I never want to end.

"This resort is big enough to hide a marching band." I chuckle; the sound is easy but hollow. Deflection has always been my shield. Inside, though, my mind churns, questions crashing like waves after the storm—relentless, inescapable.

Whatever this thing between us is, it's more than the chaos of last night. It's... forever.

She tilts her head, and I can feel the tension in her body before she speaks. "Jabari—"

"Shh." I press a finger to her lips, a move that feels less like control and more like a desperate prayer. I'm not ready to name this, to shatter the fragile peace we've found. "Don't worry, Siren. We'll talk later. I know that fascinating brain of yours is working overtime. But for now, just let me love you." My voice is low and rough, carrying more weight than I intend—like a command, a plea, and an offering rolled into one.

Her dark eyes search mine for a beat before she nods, her surrender soft and full of trust I'm not sure I deserve. And so, I flip her over and push back inside her. She's so willing and wet. Such a good girl for me.

I love her again, pouring everything I can't say into how I hold, kiss, and lose myself in her. It's wild and consuming, like how the ocean claims the shore after a storm. When our breathing evens out, reality knocks again, impatient and persistent.

I push up on my elbows, glancing down at her. "Okay, Siren. Get dressed. I'm taking you out."

Her brows lift, curiosity and a trace of mischief lighting her face. "Where are we going?"

I sit up, scrubbing a hand over my jaw. "Let's call it the Jabari Sights and Sounds Experience." The words come out with more bravado than I feel, but I force a grin, knowing she won't let me off easy. " We need to assess any storm damage anyway. Come on."

Our clothes from yesterday have dried, and she's ready in minutes. We enter the crisp morning air; the world is fresh and damp with the storm's remnants. Nothing looks out of place except for broken windows, natural debris, and tree branches strewn about. That storm's bark was worse than its bite.

Chesapeake Heights sweeps before us, a patchwork of memories I've tried to outrun. Each step feels heavier, and each landmark is a ghost calling my name.

"See that pier?" I nod toward the weathered wood jutting into the bay. "Caught my first fish there. Thought I was king of the world."

Her laugh is light and teasing, her hand brushing mine. "Bet you were adorable with your little fishing rod."

"Adorable?" I scoff, side-eyeing her with mock indignation. "Not in my vocabulary, Siren."

Her laughter dances around us, and it's enough to keep the ghosts at bay for a moment. Then her eyes find mine, steady and full of something I can't name. "Jabari Freeman, King of the Bay," she murmurs, her tone laced with challenge.

"King, Emperor, or Chief. Depends on the day," I say, my voice dropping. Her lightness answers my darkness, but I wonder how long she'll keep holding on when she realizes how heavy my reality is.

We walk on, the silence stretching but never uncomfortable. I point out the oak tree where my initials are carved, the steps of the chapel where I once prayed for courage before being deployed, and the cracks in the sidewalk that hold more of my truth than I care to admit. Each place is a piece of me, a history hidden behind ambition and duty.

"I don't want you to leave, Jabari," Sierra says softly, her hand slipping into mine. Her fingers tighten, a lifeline in the chaos I've spent my life navigating alone. "Stay here with me."

I glance at her, her face open, her voice daring me to let her in. "Careful what you wish for, Siren. You might get it." My words carry a warning, but as I look at her, a small part of me hopes she'll call my bluff.

"Tell me," She whispers. Tell me why you run from this place. I know it can't all be tied up in your ex.

I nod. "Right here," I say, my voice rough, the words snagging on the edges of something I can't quite name. "This is where my father brought me after I told him I wanted to be a soldier." The confession falls between us, heavy like the tide pulling back. "I was twelve. He said my life wasn't mine to decide. That serving Chesapeake Heights was my blood, my duty. The only job I'd ever have after Morehouse, and giving Uncle Sam four years, was CEO of the Chesapeake Heights Resort."

The air feels thicker now, weighted by memories I've spent years trying to outrun. I glance at Sierra, bracing for pity or unease. Instead, her freckled face is calm, her wild auburn curls framing eyes that see far too much. She nods, her voice soft and steady. "That's a lot for a kid to carry."

Her words hit somewhere deep, loosening something I didn't know was still clenched. "Envy isn't in my nature," I say, my gaze fixed on the horizon. "But sometimes, I look at people who just... get to choose, and I'm jealous. I've always wanted that freedom. In a way, what Vee did freed me. It gave me an excuse to buck tradition and do what I wanted. So, running Chesapeake Heights feels like I'm folding on my freedom." I grab her and kiss her knuckles. "It feels like I'm giving up my right to choose. But then there's you..."

She doesn't flinch or try to smooth over the bitterness in my voice. Instead, she slips her hand into mine, her fingers threading through mine like they belong there. "You're choosing now, Jabari. You chose to bring me here to share this with me."

Her words strike a chord I'm not ready to face. I let out a dark and sharp laugh, more at myself than anything. "Feels less like sharing and more like confessing sins."

We fall into step, our footprints trailing behind us as the waves lap at the shore. I gesture toward the rickety pier in the distance, weathered by time and salt water. "See that? My father taught me to crab there. He told me patience was the key to everything. What he didn't mention was how infuriating patience could be."

"Sounds like you were a regular Poseidon." She squeezes my hand, her laughter weaving warmth into the cold memories.

"Yeah, well, not quite. I didn't ever catch much. But, it taught me how to sit still and wait." I glance at her, my voice dropping. "Guess that came in handy as a SEAL. But waiting doesn't mean much if you can't decide what you're waiting for. Or where you want to plant yourself."

Her steps falter, her gaze finding mine, wide and open. "Jabari... Stay." Her voice is barely above a whisper, but there's no mistaking the understanding in her tone, the weight of her unspoken words.

I guide Sierra to a picnic area nestled beneath the shade of sprawling oaks. The towering trees whisper in the breeze, their leaves rustling like they carry secrets too heavy to keep. The burden of their knowing settles on my shoulders, stirring memories I've buried for years.

"Jabari, this place is special," Sierra's voice trails off, but the reverence in her tone says enough. She feels it too—the pull of history, the echoes of a time when life was simpler and far more complicated.

"We used to come here after church," I say, nodding toward a weathered picnic table. Its surface is etched with Vee's and my initials in a carved promise, a testament to youthful hope and the inevitability of time. "Family tradition. But it's also where I learned that love can be a cruel joke."

"Your past relationship?" Her hand finds mine, warm and

steady, pulling me back to the present. Her voice is soft, but there's no pity—just a quiet invitation for honesty.

"Yeah. The grand betrayal." My laugh is bitter, sharp enough to cut through the nostalgia hanging in the air. "Serving overseas, you see some messed-up things, but nothing quite prepares you when your ex-fiancée gets married under the same oak tree where you proposed. I know she found comfort in someone else's bed while I was dodging bullets, but why did she feel the need to twist the knife?"

"Jabari, I'm so sorry." There's steel beneath her sympathy, a strength that catches me off guard. It's the sound of someone who's been through their wars and come out swinging.

I look at her, a wry smile tugging at my lips. "Guess we've both danced with devils, huh?"

"More like a tango with trust issues." Her laugh is short, almost self-deprecating, softening something jagged in me. "The only other man I gave my heart to was my college sweetheart. He strung me along for years before picking some rich girl he grew up with. His family had arranged the marriage since they were kids, and he knew it. But he still let me believe we'd be married one day."

I turn and place my hands on her shoulders, and I see the hurt that bastard caused. No wonder she has such a hard time trusting and leaning on me. I'm another rich boy with lots of promises. He needs to pay.

Without an inch of amusement, I ask her, "Do you want me to kill him? Just give me his name, Siren. He'll be gone by midnight."

She laughs until she looks into my eyes. When she sees I'm serious, she smacks my chest. "No, Jabari! What the hell? You can't kill anyone for me."

"Tuh," I scoff. "I can and will if you ask me to. Siren, I've killed many people in my line of work, and one more on my score sheet won't phase God or the devil. You keep that in mind."

She shakes her head in disbelief and speaks. "Anyway..."

I smirk. "Anyway, trust is an intricate dance." I tug her into a loose embrace, holding her close amid the ghosts of cookouts and Sunday afternoons. Her head rests against my chest, and for a fleeting moment, the weight of the past feels bearable. "Maybe it's time to change the steps."

"Yes, please," she agrees, quiet but resolute.

I pull back abruptly, the motion more reflexive than intentional. "Let's move. I have one more thing to show you." I don't want to linger here, where the past feels too alive, too suffocating.

We walk along the dirt path, the sun weaving in and out of the clouds above. It's not long before we reach a clearing bordered by wildflowers and the remnants of my childhood fortress—a tree house, crooked and leaning but still standing after all these years and many storms.

"I built this with my brothers." A low chuckle escapes me, tinged with the memory of scraped knees and arguments over who got the hammer. "Our castle in the sky."

"It's beautiful," Sierra says, her head tilted as she studies the faded planks. "Looks like it could use a little love, though."

"Life's been a bit rough on it," I admit, my eyes tracing the familiar lines of the structure. "Kinda like us."

"Think you'll ever rebuild it?" There's a spark in her eyes, a challenge I hadn't expected, and it sends a jolt straight through me.

"Maybe." I run a hand along the worn ladder, the wood rough beneath my fingers. "With the right partner, it might be worth the risk."

"Building something lasting?" Her voice is soft, but her question lands like a dare.

"Something like that." The words hang in the air between us, fragile but hopeful.

"Then count me in," she says, and I know she's not just talking about the tree house.

"Careful, Siren." A half smile tugs at my lips as I meet her gaze. "I might just hold you to that."

"Good." Her fingers squeeze mine, her expression steady and sure. "Because I'm not going anywhere, Jabari Freeman. And neither are you."

Her words settle deep, filling spaces I hadn't realized were empty. I test the ladder with cautious steps, and when it holds, I climb with more confidence than I've felt in years. The platform creaks beneath my weight, the sound a mix of defiance and resilience. Sierra follows her laugh, a melody that carries through the air, breathing life into this forgotten relic.

"Watch your step," I warn, half teasing. "Can't have you breaking your neck on my account."

"Relax, Jabari. My guardian angel's got me," she says, her tone playful as she quickly steps onto the platform.

"Guardian angel, huh?" I lean against the wall, watching her take it all in. "Guess that makes me holy by association."

"Or just stick with me," she counters, her eyes sparkling with mischief.

"Stuck or blessed?" I murmur, the humor giving way to something quieter, more serious. "Never thought I'd find someone who could climb into my past and make it feel like it's worth staying there for a while."

Her eyes soften, her arms folding across her chest. "Jabari Freeman, are you getting sentimental on me?"

"Maybe I am, Siren." The nickname falls quickly from my lips, a natural fit. "There's something about you... something that makes me want to share more than just stories."

"Is that so?" Her voice wavers just enough to hint at her fears.

I reach for her hand, my fingers brushing hers. The contact is electric, grounding me even as it sends my heart racing. "I don't know much about destiny, but I know I've never been surer of anything than I am about this. About us. I love you, and if you'll have me, I'll spend the rest of my days ensuring you know you have the keys to my kingdom. My heart lies with you."

Her breath catches, and she steps closer, her voice barely a whisper. "You make the ground feel solid, Jabari. Even when everything else is up in the air, I'll have you now and choose you daily for the rest of our lives."

The weight of her confession pulls us closer, the air thick with unspoken promises. And then, the space between us disappears. Our lips meet, and the kiss is everything—fire and tenderness, passion and vulnerability. It's the kind of kiss that changes things, that sets a course you can't turn back from.

In the heart of an old tree house, surrounded by memories of who I was, Sierra Watson makes me believe in who I could be. And for the first time, I see a future built on something unshakable: us.

TWENTY-SEVEN

Endless Love

SIERRA AND JABARI

SIERRA

In the aftermath of the lifelong promise Jabari and I made to each other, I find myself back at the Baycrest, lingering in the doorway of the sunroom. I'll meet him and his family for dinner in the main dining room in an hour. But I wanted to check in on my sister first.

Amara and Shana practice yoga and their movements are fluid and synchronized like they are two parts of the same story. Sometimes, I feel a sharp twinge of jealousy watching them. Amara has connected with my sister in ways I couldn't, and their bond grows daily.

Lately, they've seemed more like sisters than Shana and me.

I mentioned it to Amara last week, and my words were tinged with frustration and hurt. She'd only smiled, her tone patient but firm. "Shana and I connect out of necessity. Familiar battles. I've had my demons to fight," she said cryptically. I didn't press her. Her secrets are hers to keep.

"Focus on your breathing, Shana," Amara says now, her voice steady and commanding. It's the kind of voice that doesn't ask—it tells. "You're not just healing your body; you're reclaiming your life."

Shana nods from her yoga mat, her body trembling with effort. Sweat glistens on her temples, but her jaw is set with determination. Every movement feels like a declaration of defiance against the demons that have haunted her.

"Your determination is stronger than your addiction," Amara continues, her gaze unwavering.

"Remember that."

The word *addiction* lodges in my chest like a shard of ice. It brings back that moment two weeks ago, in Baycrest's foyer, the day Shana lashed out and cursed me, told me she wished she'd thrown me away. The memory lives rent-free in my mind, an uninvited guest I can't evict. But Amara got through to her that day in a way I couldn't. She convinced Shana to go back to the infirmary to admit she was spiraling.

Through Amara's support, Shana confessed she'd been abusing alcohol again, her anxiety and depression swallowing her whole. The psychologist at Baycrest called her outburst more than a mental breakdown—a cry for help.

I watch them now, an invisible spectator to their quiet recovery dance. The air between them is charged, alive with the electricity of shared pain and unspoken understanding. Amara's arena is one of tough love and empathy, and Shana rises to meet her every challenge.

"Good. Now hold it... and release," Amara instructs. Shana exhales loudly, the sound like a physical surrender. For the first time in a long while, the weight on her shoulders seems to ease.

"Thank you," Shana murmurs, her voice fragile but genuine.

"Thank yourself," Amara replies, her smile soft and proud. "You're doing the work."

Shana's eyes flick to me, and before I can retreat into the shadows, she calls out, "Sierra, come here."

I freeze, torn between fear and hope, but I force myself forward. We haven't talked since that day she lost her damn mind. I've been too scared—of her anger, of my helplessness.

"Amara, can you give us a minute?" Shana asks.

"Of course," Amara replies, rolling up her mat with practiced ease. As she passes me, she rubs my arm—a small gesture of reassurance that I cling to

Shana pats the spot next to her on the mat, and I sit, the tension between us thick and unyielding.

"Sierra," she starts, her voice unsteady, her hands fidgeting with the edge of her towel. "I need to talk to you."

I nod, my voice caught in my throat. "You don't have to explain, Shana. I understand you were going through—"

"No," she cuts me off, her tone firm but breaking. "I *do* need to explain. I need to say this." She inhales sharply, steadying herself. "I'm sorry. For what I said, for how I acted. That day at Baycrest... I didn't mean it. Any of it." Her voice cracks, and her gaze drops to her hands. "I was hurting, and I lashed out."

The words hang between us, heavy with the weight of their truth.

"You're the most important person in my life, Sierra," she continues, her voice gaining strength. "I've never regretted taking care of you. Not for a single moment."

Tears burn at the edges of my eyes, but I blink them away, determined to stay steady for her. "I know," I whisper. "I've always known. Even when it hurt, I never doubted your love."

Shana exhales shakily, and for a moment, she looks smaller,

like the weight she's carried for so long is finally too much. "With Amara's help, I've realized I can't do this alone. I've made a decision—I'm going to rehab."

Her words hit me like a wave, knocking the air from my lungs. Rehab. The word is terrifying and hopeful, a beacon of light and an acknowledgment of darkness.

"That's brave, Shana," I say, my voice thick with emotion. "Incredibly brave. And I'll be with you every step of the way. You're not alone in this."

Her lips tremble into a smile as tears spill over. When I reach for her, she doesn't hesitate, folding into my arms like we're kids again, clinging to each other against the world. She pulls back and wipes her eyes. "Please tell Jabari I said thank you for paying my debt and loving you. I can tell he adores you. Don't be afraid to take that leap, sis."

I wipe my eyes, too. "Oh, I'm jumping in with both feet. Have you seen that man? He is fine!" We both laugh, and I've got my sister back for the first time in what feels like forever.

* * *

JABARI

The dining room hums with life, a symphony of clattering silverware and hushed conversations. The familiar scene tugs at something deep in my chest, a mix of nostalgia and pride. My gaze settles on Malik and Mama, their heads bent close over a pile of papers and a laptop that has seen better days. Ma's infamous top bun bounces as she nods emphatically. Malik's gestures, like his ideas, need more space than his words can provide.

I squeeze Sierra's hand and brush a kiss against her cheek as we step further inside. Her smile anchors me, a quiet reassurance amid a life that's been anything but simple lately.

"Look at this photo from the sixties," Malik says, his finger tracing the screen like he's touching a piece of history. "Man, if these walls could talk..."

"Focus, Malik," Ma chides gently, though her eyes shine with a shared reverence. "We need to make the preservation society see why this history isn't just important—it's essential. Remember Maya's notes. Stick to the guidelines."

Adom's wife, Maya, had been a godsend, organizing the chaos of our family's stories into something coherent during the storm. She'd spent hours with my mom, teasing out details, connecting dots, and turning memories into a case for legacy. Anyone who doubts the strength of Black networks has never seen how far ours stretches. Across continents, across struggles —it's always there when you need it.

"Right, right," Malik says, grinning, his rebel spirit momentarily tamed. "Let's give them the old Freeman razzle-dazzle."

Ma's laughter bubbles up, warm and genuine, loosening a knot of tension I hadn't realized I was holding. They're a mother-and-son team tied by blood and an unyielding dedication to our history. I still don't understand Malik or his methods. He was a damn good Ranger; his medal cabinet rivals mine. Then, one day, he stepped away from all of it. I pray that one day, we'll be in a space where he feels he can confide in me.

"Chesapeake Heights isn't just a place," Ma says, tapping the text on their presentation. "It's a heartbeat. It's where our people danced, loved, and rose above hate."

"Sounds like you're pitching a romance novel, not a historic landmark," Malik quips, though the pride in his voice is unmistakable.

"Of course," Ma fires back, her conviction wrapping around her words like armor. "Because every good story has heart—and ours will beat loud and clear for anyone willing to listen."

I watch them. Their dynamic blends banter and purpose,

and I know they'll handle it no matter how brutal this fight might be. In our family, when we fight, we fight to win.

"Hey, Jabari, you gonna stand there daydreaming, or will you help us save history?" Malik calls out, dragging me back to the present.

"Wouldn't miss it for the world," I reply, my resolve hardening. Control might be an illusion, but legacy? That's something real. Something worth holding on to.

As the dining room transforms for dinner, the silverware clatters, and the conversation hums, wrapping me like a warm blanket. The Freeman family dinner is in full swing, with laughter and teasing filling the space. I glance at Sierra, sitting across from me, her smile bright and soft in the flickering candlelight. My stomach knots, but it's not nerves from battle or danger—it's the anticipation of what's to come.

"Jabari, you've been unusually quiet tonight," Malik says, raising a suspicious brow.

"Maybe he's just savoring Marty's cooking," Ma offers diplomatically, though the glint in her eye tells me she knows better.

"Or," Amara adds, her tone softer but no less insistent, "he's got something on his mind."

"All right, all right." I clear my throat, the weight of leadership pressing down on me. "There's no easy way to say this, so —here it is."

Sierra's fingers slip into mine under the table, steady and sure. Her quiet strength lends me the courage I didn't realize I needed.

"Sierra and I—we're together. And I'm staying here with her."

The table falls silent, the air thick with anticipation. Then, as if on cue, Amara bursts out, "Finally!"

Her exclamation sets off a wave of laughter and applause.

"About damn time," Malik adds, grinning wide enough to split his face. "I thought you'd dance around each other forever."

"Leave it to Jabari to turn romance into a strategic operation," Amara teases, her eyes twinkling.

"Does this mean we'll see little Freemans running around soon?" Malik asks, ever the instigator.

"Give them some time, son," Mama cuts in, her gentle scolding tempered by the joy shining in her eyes. "They've got to get married first." She winks in my direction.

Sierra's composure is unshaken as she smiles. "We're taking it one step at a time."

"Smart girl," Amara says, her approving look layered with understanding. "I'm sure you both have everything under control."

"Control is an illusion, remember?" I add, trying to match the lightness of their banter. "But with Sierra, I don't mind letting go a little."

"Aw, our fearless leader has a soft side," Amir coos mockingly.

"Guess love's the one battle even a Navy SEAL can't win," Asa teases.

"Love isn't a battlefield," I say, surprising even myself with the truth of it. "It's home."

The words hang in the air, softening the laughter and shifting the mood. Sierra squeezes my hand, her freckles like a constellation of promises between us.

"I like the sound of that," she says, her voice low but sure.

"Welcome to the chaos, Sierra," Amara says warmly. "You're one of us now."

"Thank you," Sierra replies, her voice thick with emotion. "It feels like where I'm meant to be."

The rest of the evening unfolds as a symphony of stories, laughter, and plans for the future. Something shifts inside me through it all—a release I hadn't known I needed. Maybe control is really overrated. Perhaps the real strength lies in surrendering to the unpredictable tides of love and family.

"Here's to new beginnings," I toast, raising my glass.

"To the family," they echo, and at that moment, I know: this is what we've been fighting for all along. This is home.

Epilogue

JABARI

SIERRA STEPS INTO VIEW, AND FOR A MOMENT, TIME stops.

My soon-to-be wife moves with the grace of a goddess, each step deliberate, each breath weaving a spell that snares me whole. My heart hammers against my ribcage, so loud it drowns out the soft murmur of our gathered family and friends.

Her auburn curls catch the fading sunlight, framing her face like a halo of fire. That smile—a quiet yet devastating curve of her lips—turns my legs to stone and my chest to ash.

That same smile brought this battle-hardened Navy SEAL to his knees, forcing me to lay down every weapon I've ever known.

"Damn, she's fine," I murmur under my breath. It's half prayer, half curse because how do I deserve someone like her?

The ivory lace of her dress clings to her curves like it's been designed to worship her, each intricate detail amplifying the truth I've known since the moment we met. She isn't just beautiful—she's radiant. But it's more than the dress, more than her elegance. It's the strength behind the beauty. Sierra Watson, my Siren, has stared down the demons of her sister's struggles and walked unscathed through the storms of her past. She's everything I never dared to ask for.

Our love hasn't been easy, but it's been worth every fight, every scar, every late-night conversation where we picked through our pasts piece by piece to make room for this. Together, we built a foundation stronger than the tides. A house in Annapolis, close enough to Chesapeake Heights for family but far enough for just us. She traded her school counseling job for a role here as our on-site wellness director, but she's also training to be a historian, thanks to Maya Annan's help. This partnership we've built—it's the heart of who we are.

As I watch Sierra close the distance between us, my chest tightens at how close I came to losing her, to letting fear win.

When she reaches me, our eyes lock, and in that silent moment, every vow I've rehearsed passes between us without a word. Stronger than anything printed in the carefully crafted programs tucked into everyone's hands.

"Jabari Freeman," the officiant prompts, pulling me back from the brink of memory.

I take a breath, steadying the storm inside me. "I, Jabari," I begin, my voice steady even as my heart races, "take you, Sierra, to be my life partner. I've seen darkness, but you're the dawn after the longest night. You're the laughter in an empty house, the calm in my storm. And I promise, Siren, to be the man who stands by you through every flood and tempest."

Her hand is steady in mine, but her eyes undo me. They're brimming with emotion, pools of hope, vulnerability, and fierce love. I see every tear unshed, every battle fought, and every victory won in her gaze.

"Jabari," she begins, her voice soft but steady, wrapping around me like a melody I've been waiting my whole life to hear. "I take you with all your shadows and light. I vow to be the shore you can always return to, your sanctuary when the echoes of war get too loud. Together, we rise above every challenge. Your battles are mine, and our victories will always be shared."

"Through hell and high water," I add, letting a smirk pull at the corner of my mouth. It's dark humor, our private joke, born from the chaos of a literal storm that forced us to lean into each other or be swept away.

"Especially through high water," Sierra replies, her laugh light but grounding, her thumb brushing over my knuckles. It's a slight touch, but it's enough to tether me, to remind me that I'm home in her hands.

We've danced through debts and disasters, tempted fate in ways neither of us could've predicted. And yet, here we stand, exchanging rings that carry more weight than anything I've ever held. Because this—this is the fight I choose. This is the victory I'll never stop fighting for.

As I slide the ring onto her finger and feel the cool metal of hers settle onto mine, the world fades. It's just us, two warriors who've found peace in each other.

I know one thing with absolute certainty: Sierra is my forever, and nothing will ever take her from me.

After a few more words spoken over us, the officiant's voice cuts through all the noise with the only words I want to hear.

"I now pronounce you husband and wife. You may kiss your bride."

I take Sierra's face in my hands, my thumbs brushing against the soft curve of her cheekbones, and kiss her like it's the first time again. Our lips meet, slow and deliberate, and when our tongues touch, they dance in sync—like they've known each other's rhythm for a lifetime. The kiss deepens, and my need rises, sharp and undeniable. I'm unsure I'll make it to the reception without tasting her everywhere.

She senses my intent, laughing softly against my mouth. Her voice drops to a whisper that only I can hear. "No, sir. You'll have to wait until tonight. We've got guests to entertain."

I groan in protest but force myself to let go. The promise in her eyes is enough to keep me at bay—for now. I clasp her hand and lift it high as the officiant introduces us as husband and wife.

"Ladies and gentlemen, Mr. and Mrs. Jabari Freeman."

The crowd cheers, their applause mingling with the soft rhythm of waves lapping against the shore. The sun dips low, casting its final amber rays over Chesapeake Bay, painting the scene in hues of gold and fire. The heavens have conspired to shine a celestial spotlight on Sierra and me. A gentle breeze teases the hem of her dress, carrying whispers from the sea that seem to bless this moment.

Instead of running down the aisle, we linger, creating a receiving line as the evening settles around us. My gaze flicks to Malik, standing tall and steady as my best man. His sharp features are carved with the kind of resolve that's carried us through storms far fiercer than anything this bay has ever seen. Over the past year, we've grown closer, unraveling parts of his past he once kept hidden. He hasn't told me everything, though —I think that's because it's not entirely his story to tell. Jade Jackson holds the key to that mystery, and I can't wait to see how it unfolds.

Malik catches my eye, a knowing smirk tugging at the corner of his mouth as if he's read every thought I've tried to hide. It's a look that says he knows what this moment means to me—the weight of it, the joy of it, the relief of finally letting go of the fears that kept me from this for so long.

Beside Sierra, Tiana is practically glowing. Her light, infectious, and unrestrained laugh fills the air, reminding me of the strength she's lent Sierra through her most brutal battles. Her pride radiates off her, a beacon of sisterhood that seems capable of moving mountains or, at the very least, weathering the heaviest storms.

Sierra's sister, Shana, stands close by, her smile quiet but steady. Six months sober, she's rebuilt her relationship with Sierra brick by brick, and I've learned to see her in a new light. It wasn't easy at first; I was angry at the pain she caused the woman I love. But I see now how far she's come, and she's earned my respect and love as a sister.

My brothers, Amir and Asa, also stand tall by my side, making this a true family affair. They say it takes a village to raise a child, but I also know it takes your village to support your love.

"Never thought I'd see the day," Malik says, leaning in, his voice low but laced with amusement. "Jabari Freeman, brought to his knees by love. Or is it just the tightness of that suit?"

I side-eye him, a grin tugging at my lips. "Watch it," I warn, the humor slipping into my voice despite myself. "Love's the one storm I don't mind getting swept up in."

"Better be," Tiana teases from across the way, her eyes sparkling with mischief. "Sierra's got enough fire to keep even your cold feet warm."

"Careful now," I shoot back, my gaze locking on Sierra's as she laughs at something her sister says. "Or I'll show the newly minted Mrs. Freeman she married a man whose feet and body are anything but cold. Right here and right now!"

The laughter that follows wraps around us softly and easily, like the sunset embracing the horizon—close, warm, and filled with unspoken gratitude. But beneath the teasing, there's something deeper, something unbreakable: a shared understanding that whatever comes next, we'll face it together. Family is our anchor, our strength.

As the sun dips below the bay and the sky surrenders to the night, I feel it in my bones: we've made it. We've found our way here through the storms, doubts, and scars that once defined us. Control isn't about holding tight to the reins; it's about knowing who's there when you let go.

And with Sierra by my side, I've never felt more at home.

The End

Thank You for Reading "Free to Fall." If you loved reading this #HappyBlackRomance as much as I did writing it, please leave a review on Amazon or Goodreads.

Amazon

GoodReads

Malik's Story is next! Stay tuned and follow me on TikTok to catch this summer's release date.

Are you on My Mailing List? Stay current on all my future releases, and join my ARC Team!

Join Mailing List

Also by Louise Lennox

ALSO BY LOUISE LENNOX

THE SEXY SOVEREIGN SERIES (ALSO ON AUDIBLE)

Craving a King: https://geni.us/CravingAKing

Choosing the Chief: https://geni.us/AdomandMaya

Possessing A Prince: https://geni.us/SenyandAbena

THE KIAWAH KISSES SERIES

Merry Kiss Me : https://geni.us/Rhueandsymone

Kiss of Life: https://geni.us/cameronandtara

Kiss of Fate : https://geni.us/Rayandnicole

Kiss of Karma: https://geni.us/Richardandkeisha

THE CHESAPEAKE HEIGHTS SERIES

Free to Fall: https://geni.us/FreetoFall

STAND-ALONE NOVELS & NOVELLAS

Savannah's Salvation: https://geni.us/MichaelandSavannah

The Wine Down: https://geni.us/RiddickandBrandi

Love & Lipstick: https://geni.us/PeterandMia

Love & Lyrics: https://geni.us/LukerandRaina

Make Me:https://geni.us/MakeMeSir

About the Author

ABOUT LOUISE LENNOX

Contemporary romance Author Louise Lennox is a hopeful romantic writing steamy romances full of heart and healing.

A Spelman College and Georgetown University graduate, Louise provides women with diverse and meaningful representation in romance novel pages. Not seeing enough women like herself headlining positive love stories, she launched #HappyBlackRomance; a community of readers and writers committed to creating and sharing positive romance stories featuring Black heroines.

Louise Lennox plots highlight the joys of Black relationships across the diaspora, pushing readers from all cultural backgrounds to admire them for their strength and downright sexiness. In her novels, sparks always fly; the sex amazes, and the characters always leave the world better than they found it through their love.

When she's not writing, Louise is enjoying her work as a school leader, wife, and mother of the two cutest dragons ever to walk the earth!

To learn more about #HappyBlackRomance and to score a free book or two, check out her website www.lovelouiselen nox.com.